Today a Woman Went Mad in the Supermarket

Fiction

An Available Man

Summer Reading

The Doctor's Daughter

Tunnel of Love

Silver

In the Palomar Arms

Hearts

In the Flesh

Ending

Nonfiction

*The Company of Writers: Fiction Workshops and
Thoughts on the Writing Life*

Books for Young Readers

Wish You Were Here

Toby Lived Here

Out of Love

Introducing Shirley Braverman

Today a Woman Went Mad in the Supermarket

Stories

Hilma Wolitzer

Foreword by Elizabeth Strout

BLOOMSBURY PUBLISHING

NEW YORK • LONDON • OXFORD • NEW DELHI • SYDNEY

BLOOMSBURY PUBLISHING
Bloomsbury Publishing Inc.
1385 Broadway, New York, NY 10018, USA

BLOOMSBURY, BLOOMSBURY PUBLISHING, and the
Diana logo are trademarks of Bloomsbury Publishing Plc

First published in the United States 2021

LIBRARY OF CONGRESS CATALOGING-IN-PUBLICATION DATA IS AVAILABLE

ISBN: HB: 978-1-63557-762-4; EBOOK: 978-1-63557-763-1

2 4 6 8 10 9 7 5 3

Typeset by Westchester Publishing Services
Printed and bound in the U.S.A. by Sheridan ,Chelsea, Michigan.

To find out more about our authors and books visit
www.bloomsbury.com
and sign up for our newsletters.

Bloomsbury books may be purchased for business or promotional use. For
information on bulk purchases please contact Macmillan Corporate and
Premium Sales Department at specialmarkets@macmillan.com.

Morty

This was the night Mrs. Bridge concluded that while marriage might be an equitable affair, love itself was not.

—EVAN S. CONNELL, *MRS. BRIDGE*

The author thanks the following magazines,
where several of these stories originally appeared
in somewhat different form:

The Saturday Evening Post, *New American Review*,
Esquire, *Ms.*, *Prairie Schooner*

CONTENTS

CONTENTS

Foreword by Elizabeth Strout

Hilma Wolitzer once told an interviewer, "I don't believe there's such a thing as ordinary life. I think all life is extraordinary."

In these immensely gratifying, poignant, funny, and well-crafted stories, you may find—at first glance—what you think of as ordinary lives, but you will come away recognizing that every person does, in fact, have an extraordinary life. Here you will see women and men who live their daily existence with all the turbulence of the unexpected, starting with the title story, "Today a Woman Went Mad in the Supermarket." The woman who goes mad will be imprinted indelibly on your brain, her two small boys clinging to her skirt ("Pee-pee," one of them whispers, before wetting himself), and there is her pocketbook, which, near the end of the story, lies on the counter—empty; it has been left there by the narrator "sneakily, as one leaves a litter of kittens in a vacant lot." In just a few pages Wolitzer reveals a glimpse of the life of this woman, her two little boys, and the husband who comes to get her. That's all we will ever know about the woman who went mad in the supermarket. But we enter the story with our own experiences and therefore make it our own. Wolitzer always leaves enough spaces between the lines for us to embrace her work in this way. This is part of her marvelousness as a writer.

It should be noted that this story was first published in the *Saturday Evening Post* in 1966. A number of these stories were published in *Esquire* in the early 1970s, and one in *Ms.* magazine, as well. All stories take place in a time in history, and Wolitzer captures that time with a breathtaking precision. But it is always—for Wolitzer— about the characters; that they lived during this time informs who they are, but their particularities make them special—extraordinary.

Wolitzer is largehearted in her work, judging no one. And she is also an exquisite craftswoman. She understands how to render the details so well that we are immediately placed inside the story. In "Bodies," the protagonist, Sharon, is unexpectedly called to fly across the country to help get her husband out of a wonderfully horrifying situation— not to be gone into here—and on the plane she sits next to a man who has had a few drinks. "He leans back in his seat and faces her intimately, as if they are sharing a bed pillow." Boom. We are right there with them.

This is another part of Wolitzer's wonder as a writer: she will start off in one place and end up in a situation one never would have imagined, and yet it ultimately makes a kind of perfect sense. The story "Overtime" is a dazzling example of this: a man's ex-wife won't leave him alone in his current marriage, and his current wife's response to this is hilarious, and also moving. The ending of this story—not to be given away here—is supreme.

As are so many of the endings; there is a little bump, and we realize we have landed safely.

This sense of safety—of being in safe hands—as we read is never to be underestimated. The reader does not have to know of this need, but the writer does. And in these stories, no matter what happens, we have the sense of safety that a great storyteller provides. Wolitzer's prose is sure-footed as it careens us through the lives of these people. In "The Sex Maniac" the narrator waits anxiously for a spotting of the man said to be a sex maniac. The first two lines read, "Everybody said that there was a sex maniac loose in the complex and I thought—it's about time. It had been a long asexual winter." Humor, always riding alongside pathos, is at play in all these stories; it is there in the safety of the narrative voice.

And there is wisdom as well. In "Mother" a woman thinks: "The very worst thing, she was certain, was not human misery, but its nakedness, and the naked witness of others." Wolitzer allows us to be that witness, but with an empathy that rises up quietly from the pages. It does not frighten us, it envelops us. This is true as we drive with Howard and his wife Paulette out to the suburbs on

Sundays to view new houses on the market; her husband is depressed and "Paulie" knows this will cheer him, as it does. It is only life, we realize. In all its extraordinariness.

Hilma Wolitzer published her first piece of work—a poem—at the age of nine. It was in a publication put out by the New York City Department of Sanitation; it was a poem about winter. She has gone on to be the author of fourteen books. As a young girl she thought of herself as a poet, but as she got older she thought of herself as a visual artist. She would sit on the subway and draw the faces of people around her on the stock market pages of the newspaper she was reading. "Everyone's face was fascinating to me, and I would wonder what their lives were like." It is this deep, abiding—extraordinary— curiosity that makes her the writer that she is.

The story "Nights" is a magnificent portrayal of a woman with insomnia. She roams through her apartment, gazes out the window, does all the things that insomniacs do. If you ever have a sleepless night, read this story first—it will make you understand you are not alone in the world. This is what literature does for us; it breaks down these barriers for a moment within which we all live. And if you are in the hands of a master storyteller, you may even have a moment of grace and think to your- self, Thank you, Hilma Wolitzer.

Thank you.

Today a Woman Went Mad
in the Supermarket

Today a Woman Went Mad in the Supermarket

E ven now, saying it aloud, or repeating that sentence to my husband later, I will see that it is meant to amuse, to attract interest, to get attention. Of course, I'm too sophisticated in things psychological (isn't everyone today?) to think that one goes mad at a moment's notice. There are insipid beginnings to a nervous breakdown. There's lonely crying in the bathroom, balanced on the edge of the tub, and in the kitchen, weeping into the dishwater, tears breaking the surface of the suds. There's forgetting, or wishing to forget, the names of the children, the way to the local bank, the reason for getting up in the morning. There's loss of vanity—toenails growing long and dirty into prehensile claws, hair uncombed, eyebrows unplucked. Yet something seems very right to me about going mad in a supermarket: those painted oranges, threatening to burst at the navel; formations of cans, armored with labels and prices and weights; cuts of meat, aggressively bloody; and crafty peaches and apples, showing only their glowing perfect faces, hiding the rot and soft spots on their undersides.

Nevertheless, this woman did not go trundling her cart through the ordered chaos. She stood transfixed, as if caught in some great thought. She was blocking the aisle.

"Excuse me," I said tentatively, hesitant and self-protective as only a woman expecting her first child can be. "Pardon me, could I just get through?"

She turned slowly, and the two small children clinging to her skirt held on and tightened the cloth across her hips. Perhaps for the glory of the retelling, I might say that she was a great beauty, that her beauty was marred (or enhanced) only by her wild expression. In truth, she was pretty in a common sort of way, with conventional hair and eyes and nose. Only what she said then stopped me from clearing my throat and asking again if she would move and let me through.

She gripped the handle of her empty cart and said, "There is no end to it." It was spoken so simply and undramatically, but with such honest conviction that for a moment I thought she was referring to the aisle of the supermarket. Perhaps it was blocked ahead of us, and she couldn't move up farther. But then she said, "I have tried and I have tried, and there is no end to it. Ask Harold. Ask anybody, ask my mother."

"Do you feel all right?" I asked. "Can I help you?" Her knuckles were white and hard as she clung to the cart. She did not answer.

I looked around me self-consciously, and then I leaned toward her and said, "Would you like to go home?"

"You know," she said severely, "that I can't go there."

Then a woman rattled her cart toward us from the other end of the aisle. "Excuse me," she called out cheerfully. "Coming through!"

"Could you go the other way?" I asked her.

"Why should I go the other way?" she demanded.

"Because this aisle is blocked," I answered, grimacing and rolling my eyes. She looked at me suspiciously and turned her cart briskly back in the other direction. A chain of voices began in the back of the store. I heard the last one call, "Mr. A! Mr. A!"

Then for a few minutes we were alone, the woman and her children and me. We stood in the supermarket as if primed for a television commercial in which the magical product would come winging from the shelves, where brand X would forever stay, unwanted and untried. The manager, Mr. A, came eagerly toward us. He is a kindly fellow, who perhaps could seem even kinder in a small, intimate grocery store. He will sprint off on a given signal and bring back the bread crumbs or the baking soda or the canned crab meat that you can't seem to find anywhere. He rubbed his hands nervously.

"How can I bear it?" the woman cried in grief.

Mr. A looked at her questioningly. "Can I get you some water?" he asked.

She didn't answer him, but covered her mouth with her hand, so that all of her anguish was concentrated in her eyes. I began to tremble, and I worried that my concern for her would somehow affect the child I was carrying. Didn't I worry two aisles back, if, when the time came, I would choose the right baby food, that my milk would flow, that I would be a wise and tranquil mother? All this time the two small children did not release their grip on their mother's skirt.

"She's very ill," I told Mr. A.

"Should I call the police?" he asked. The woman began to weep big flowing tears, and I thought then that all the priests and plumbers and policemen of the world could not stay them.

"No, no," I said quickly, looking at the children. Bending at the knees, I leaned toward the taller child. "What's your name?" I asked him. I was close enough to smell his milky breath and to see that his nose was running onto a crusty sore right under it. He turned his face away from mine and didn't answer. Feeling bolder I took the handbag that was looped over the woman's wrist, and she didn't resist me. She seemed not to notice.

"There must be something, if only I could remember," she said vaguely. The pocketbook creaked open, as if from long disuse, or like the mouth of a nervous child at the dentist's. Mr. A peered over my shoulder. There was a sweet hair tonic smell. The pocketbook was empty. We peered into it, unbelieving. It was the saddest thing I had ever seen, that empty pocketbook.

"Jeez," Mr. A whispered. But then he brightened. "Say," he said, "say, if her pocketbook's empty, then she doesn't have any car keys. She must have walked here. If she walked here, then she can't live too far."

I looked at him coldly. "Maybe she left them in the car," I said. "Or maybe she cleaned out her purse somewhere."

This deflated him for only a moment. He looked thoughtful, then called to a stock boy who had been staring at us. Mr. A sent him out into the parking lot and told him to look at the ignitions of all the cars.

"Pee-pee," said the smaller child suddenly, tugging at his mother's skirt.

"Oh," I said. "He has to go to the bathroom." I took his fist and tried to detach it from his mother's skirt. He held fast with the tenacity of a tick in a dog's coat.

"*Mama*, pee-pee," the child insisted.

"He only wants his mother to take him," I told Mr. A, and he nodded as if I were translating from a foreign language. The child stuck his thumb into his mouth and sucked greedily. When the stock boy came back he said that there weren't any cars with keys in them.

A small group of women had gathered at the end of the aisle, curiosity drawing them close, fear keeping them distant. "Do any of you know this woman?" I called to them.

They mumbled among themselves, and then a tall, rawboned woman in a Girl Scout leader uniform walked closer. "I don't *know* her—" she began, and from the rear someone called, "Why don't you look in her pocketbook?"

"I don't *know* her," the tall woman repeated, "but I know who she is." She ducked her head and then glanced up guiltily. "Her name is Shirley Lewis. Mrs. Harold Lewis," she whispered, and then fell back into the crowd of women like a frightened informer.

"But where does she live?" I asked irritably.

"Oh-oh, pee-pee," sighed the little boy, and a stream of urine, tentatively begun, ran down his leg.

"Never rush into *anything*," his mother stated. And then, nostalgically, "How nice it was to be the children!"

"Where? Where?" I snapped at the tall woman. I knew that I was vying with Mr. A. We were playing detective, savior, twenty questions, God. Who would win this terrible contest and solve the mystery and set things right again? I had a good lead. All-powerful, matriarchal, replete with swollen belly.

The woman came forward again. She mumbled an address and stepped back into the group of women. Mr. A scribbled the information in a little notebook and went to the telephone in his office. One point for Mr. A.

"Where is Harold?" I asked slyly when Mr. A had gone. Shirley Lewis looked at me with real interest. "Ha, ha," she said, and smirked, as if I had said something vulgar but worth noting. The little boy stood, straddling his puddle, miserable with his public act. I looked into my shopping cart and saw that the frozen things had begun to sweat and thaw. I was very tired. My legs were singing with fatigue. I wanted to sit down. I wanted to go home and take a bath. The woman was tiresome, the game was tedious, the supermarket was boring.

"We sat at the table," Shirley Lewis began. "My grandmother brought in the soup. It was so heavy, her hands trembled. Uncle Al brought everybody in the car. He had a Pontiac."

Mr. A came back. He was smiling. The game was over. "Her husband is home! He was sleeping; he didn't even know she was out."

"Ahhh," moaned the crowd of women, like a Greek chorus.

Soon, the husband came. He had the car, after all. The children rushed from their mother to him. Fair-weather friends, I thought. He was tall and burly. He was wearing workman's clothes, and his shoes were untied. There were sleep creases down the side of one cheek. He ignored everyone else, although we looked eagerly to him as we might to the comedy relief in a melodrama. Incredibly, he scolded the small boy for wetting his pants. To his wife, he said, "What's the *matter* with you?" and he grabbed her arm. She went with him, and then it was all over. Several women broke away from the crowd and went to the window. They watched Harold and Shirley and the children get into the car.

I looked dully into my shopping cart. It was impossible to remember the other things I had wanted to buy. Shirley Lewis's pocketbook lay gaping on top of my own. I wondered if it would ever be returned to her. I thought that we would not be hearing from her or her husband. Harold hadn't said thank you to anyone. I imagined, giddily, an engraved card coming in the mail: "Mr. Harold Lewis and family thank you for the kindness extended to Mrs. Lewis in her time of need."

Mr. A was extremely gracious. He guided me to an unopened checkout counter and personally rang up the few items in my cart. "Some fun," he said, clucking his tongue. "You were swell." He was the master detective congratulating the cop on the beat. His munificence knew no bounds. He offered to take my package to the car.

"No, no," I said, yawning in his face. I left the pocketbook on his counter, sneakily, as one leaves a litter of kittens in a vacant lot.

"Good-bye," some of the women called to me. I had proved myself after all, and someday they would ask me to join committees and protest groups and the PTA. I went home. My matriarchal stature had changed to a pregnant waddle. When my husband came home from work, I was sitting in the bathtub and weeping.

"What—what is it?" he cried, primed for catastrophe.

"Everything," I said, gesturing at the swelling that rose above the water level. "Everything. The human condition. The world."

His face relaxed slightly, and he waited for me to go on.

I rose, the water spiraling from my belly. "A woman went mad in the supermarket today."

He managed to look both compassionate and questioning. "What did you do?"

I waved the towel as if it were a banner, a piece of evidence. "There was nothing I could do. Nothing at all. I mean, I tried, but there was simply no way that I could help her."

He took the towel and began to dry my back.

"I think I know how you feel," he said, "but you can't mother the whole world."

"No," I said. "I guess I can't, can I?" I turned around and threw myself awkwardly into his arms.

(1966)

Waiting for Daddy

T ootsie," my grandmother used to say, "he isn't coming back." She said it often, the way one repeats a popular slogan. She seemed very intuitive then, because I hardly asked about my father. Somehow she had read my mind: I believed that he would come back.

There is something terrific about not knowing your father because it opens up possibilities that just aren't there with a real mass in your mother's bed, with a father who hangs his coat in the closet at night as proof of his whereabouts. My inventions of him were generous and he was invariably handsome and misjudged. Oh, how he came back again and again—as salesmen, doctors, soldiers. His voice was the voice of every radio announcer, and I would stare into the orange moon of the radio dial and will him into knowing that I was there, sweet with forgiveness.

"He's not coming back," my grandmother whispered, and her words were followed by a haze of smoke from her Lucky Strike, like the trail after skywriting.

In those vaporous days we moved often, and I worried that he would be unable to find us, and that even if he could, everything and everyone would be changed beyond the seduction that memory can work. As I grew older I began to question my mother but she seemed to suffer from a loss of time. "He just vanished," my mother explained. It was a whole era about which I knew nothing, when men did that sort of thing, slipping away with a certain ease that eluded the law and feelings of guilt.

"You don't know anything about it," my grandmother said, and I thought that she was probably right. Yet I wanted to know, and I watched my mother, that blonde, skateless Sonja Henie, sitting in her blue dress on the edge of her bed, perched nervously as if she were on a moving vehicle. Blue was her favorite color and she and my grandmother always spent lots of time assessing other favorites—favorite vocalists, favorite flowers, favorite songs. I wondered: If Russ Columbo is her favorite vocalist, what is his favorite color, and Fred Astaire's and Leslie Howard's, and would they all love my mother in her blue dress? And would my father love her, too, if they could begin again somewhere in some other, more favorable, time?

My mother and my grandmother seemed to have no need for men. They supported us modestly with work they did in the kitchen. Sometimes they typed addresses on envelopes, facing each other at rented typewriters in the style of those twin-piano virtuosos who were so popular in the forties. They did whatever was available— pasting feathers on Kewpie dolls, stuffing circulars into those typed envelopes, or cementing silver-and-gilt hearts to greeting cards. Our wishes speed across the miles, we wish you happiness on your day, God bless your brand-new baby boy. Their kitchen was full of piecework and vague hope for the future.

Sometimes I made use of the fathers of friends. Not that those selfish girls were really willing to share. But there were times when I sat next to real fathers in movie theaters, with the exquisite texture of a man's coat brushing my arm. And I listened to the sounds of their voices with the happiness of a dog that has no use for words but is desperately alert to tone and pitch and timbre.

I began to understand about the injustices in a world where loyal and willing girls were abandoned and others, faithless and disagreeable, were not. Nothing was fair— certainly not the burden of dreams.

The dreams of my father began to change. They became sad visions of lost men on maritime ships or men huddled in bad neighborhoods, the poor clucks who die in war movies, who get kayoed in minor boxing events. Take that, I thought, and that and that. Oh, I'd punish him, see that he was lonely cuddling some tired woman in a furnished room.

All the time I kept changing right along with my conclusions. I looked into mirrors and I assessed myself in the way that a soldier assesses his weapons: fair skin, light hair, and the intensity that I felt burning through my pallor. I think that boys saw this as a kind of wildness, something hot and exciting. They pursued me and girls did not.

My mother and grandmother, who watched the hair-combing, mistook it for vanity. They approved. Vanity in a girl of my age was cute and appealing.

In high school, I met a boy named Arnie Ford and it wasn't hard to fall into step with that part of my life. "Baby baby," Arnie said. "Baby baby," with a compelling finger-snapping rhythm. I was drawn into the back seat of his father's green Chevy, and the texture of those seat covers will stay in my head forever.

Whenever I see teenagers walking, hooked together in that peculiar meshing way—arms looped around waists, necks, shoulders—I remember Arnie, who was first. It seemed strange that I could do all those things with him, discover all those sensations and odors and that new voice that came from the dark pit of my throat (Don't—oh yes, oh God) and that my mother and grandmother didn't know. In their world there could be mingling without coupling, kisses without tongues. They sat at the kitchen table earning our living. I walked past them, struck with experience, and they yoo-hooed and advised me to take some milk and cupcakes before I went to sleep.

Lying in bed, I thought about the slow passage of sperm—the mere chance of it—the rendezvous of sperm and egg like some unlikely event. I fell asleep trying to remember the beginning of myself. Later I awoke, startled, and I could hear my grandmother coughing her cigarette cough in the other room and my mother murmuring to the movie stars in her dreams. Then I remembered Arnie and the way he clicked on the overhead light in the Chevy to check for stains on the seats. I shielded my eyes against the intrusive glare and I didn't look at him.

"Okay," he announced. "All clear," as if I cared about that car.

"Shut off the light," I said, and Arnie laughed. "Hey, do you know I love you?" he said, and he turned the motor over. The smell of the exhaust overwhelmed the odors of our bodies, and then he took me home.

"What do you and Arnie talk about?" my mother asked once. She knew what we talked about—in her mind's eye she saw Mickey Rooney and Deanna Durbin movies and balloons of innocent conversation floating over our heads like halos.

But I don't remember too many things that Arnie and I actually said to each other beyond the outcries of sexual discovery. We were like two earnest workmen, intent on getting the job done. "I love you," he said. I remember *that* because he said it over and over again with liturgical zeal, fogging the windows of the car with his breath. If he said it for my sake, he didn't have to. Just his presence, the evidence of his shirt, his shoes, his comb, eased a longing I could never describe.

I told Arnie that my father was dead. It seemed to be a sensible lie at the time and it gave me a chance to consider that possibility. A dead father was a father punished beyond mercy. A dead father evaded my illusions with the cunning of a con man. What more could I do to him? I decided to let him live and I would let Arnie love me up in the dark. I would let my mother and grandmother be the way they wanted to be, too.

But the weight of judgment and choice became too much for me. My pallor became ghostly, my hands trembled at simple tasks. I thought: if my father were here, he would be my defender and my strength. But there was no one to protect me from my own bad decisions, no one to lead me from the back seats of cars.

Slowly, in the fixed pattern of my life, the groping and touching of hands and mouths became dogged ritual.

"Relax, Sandy, oh baby, just relax," Arnie begged. I could see the silver shadow of perspiration on his forehead. "I *love* you," he insisted, but it wasn't any use.

"I'm sorry," I whispered.

"You're just in a bad mood," he said hopefully, and he patted my knee and took me home.

"The lovebirds!" my grandmother cried out when she saw us. A cigarette hung from the corner of her mouth and a small burst of sparks fell to the table.

Arnie allowed his mouth to move into a little smile. He was not yet used to the ironies of life.

I sent him home and then I went into the dark retreat of my bedroom and lay across the bed with my clothes on. I could hear the shuffling rustle of cards from the kitchen where my mother and grandmother were playing rummy. I was tired. I won't think, I said to myself. I won't think about anything. But I thought of my father and that I would never know him, and my heart banged shut on the knowledge. I thought of my mother and I wanted to blame her, but she never believed she had driven him away. It was the decade, it was the climate, it was their astrological destiny.

I stood up and went into the kitchen.

"Knock with four," my grandmother said.

"You got me," my mother answered.

"Listen," I said, "did you ever hear from my father?"

"But he vanished!" my mother cried out.

"He was somewhere," I persisted. "He had to be somewhere."

"Look, he disappeared," my grandmother said severely. I was a sadistic playmate, bullying her blameless child. "It was different then. He disappeared from the face of the earth."

They exchanged pleased smiles. They were in love with the drama of their words. Gone! Vanished! My father's absence was a religious phenomenon.

"What did you do with his clothes?" I said.

They stared at me.

"What did you do with my father's clothes?"

"I don't remember," my mother said.

"I mean did you burn them or did you give them away? Did you sell them?"

"Sa-ay," my grandmother began, threatening. She half-rose from her chair.

But my mother still sat there and there were tears in her eyes. "It was such a long time ago," she said.

"It's all right," I said. "Forget it."

"The styles were different then," she said, and her brow folded.

"Sure, how could you remember?" I squeezed her arm.

"Vests, double-breasted suits," she said.

"Yes." I leaned against the sink and shut my eyes.

"Do you feel okay?" my grandmother asked.

I opened my eyes and smiled at them. "Me? I feel great," I said. I went to the window and looked out at the starless night until I found him. Then I let him go, out of that furnished room, out of that bad neighborhood. I returned him to a decent bed, shooting his seed like comets into the universe.

(1971)

Photographs

We were married in those dark ages before legalized abortion. I know that's no excuse. There were always illegal abortions. But my social circles were limited and unsophisticated. The doctors in my life were of the old-fashioned, tongue-depressor variety, who probably accepted kickbacks on unnecessary, but lawful, hysterectomies.

I knew vaguely about worldlier women who flew down to Puerto Rico and other tropical places to have safe, painless surgery and probably even had time to get in a little sun and to dance the carioca. But I had never even been in an airplane. And the stories I knew by heart were of hapless girls in the back rooms of drugstores after hours, whose blood came in fountains; poor butchered girls whose parts were packaged and distributed among the trash cans of the city.

My mother dreamed of being a grandmother someday. It appeared to be her goal in life. She wanted to wear a gold charm bracelet dangling with symbols that commemorated the births of babies. She wanted an accordion folder of photographs, that first-class ticket to the society of grandmothers.

I was born late in her life and was an only child, having denied passage to any future brothers and sisters. My mother claimed that a few months after I was born, everything had simply fallen out of her one day. As a young, misinformed girl, I had pictured the worst: a giblet tangle of fallopian tubes, ovaries, and the little pear-shaped uterus lying useless on the bathroom floor. But first I had been born, dropped in agony like an oversized egg from a disconsolate chicken. And, way behind schedule, my mother was impatient for the natural progression of events.

When I was twenty, my goal was to lie meshed with Howard forever. Sex, which I had discovered like everyone else, in the misery of childhood, had finally advanced to the ultimate stage of partnership. And what a partner I had! I recognized with awe the glorious territory we had discovered together in such blind and blundering exploration.

Later, lying in bed alone, "in trouble" already, I kept a wad of Kleenex and a flashlight for undercover checking. Nothing. There was probably still a chance that I was mistaken, or that my body was only giving me some punitive suspense. As I had assured Howard, it was my safe time, and our pleasure didn't have to be deferred for the sake of caution. Of course, he had hardly waited anyway, had barely missed a stroke.

I checked again, the flashlight locked between my knees. Nothing.

Howard advised hot baths. He lent me weights to lift. We ran together, forty laps around a school track in a neutral neighborhood, and then collapsed, panting, in the high grass behind it. All the evidence was in.

"What do you want to do?" he asked.

"You know," I said. "What about you?"

His eyes shifted restlessly, and I imagined my mother's pride and joy, a slender gelatinous thread riding the sewer currents of Queens.

"Are you afraid, Paulie?" Howard asked, and I knew then that he was.

I made him say it anyway. "Of what?" I asked, forcing his glance.

"Of . . . I don't know . . . of complications."

"Aren't you?" I said. What a mess it could be! I concentrated, forcing terrible mental pictures at him, *Daily News* headlines, even threw in some war atrocities for good measure.

He shuddered, receiving my message. I couldn't help thinking that men whose mothers have established an early habit of guilt in them are probably the easiest.

"So that's it," Howard said, and we were engaged.

I threw my arms around him, sealing the bond. "It will be wonderful," I promised. "We'll have a wonderful life together. We'll have terrific good luck. I can feel it."

He hugged me back, but all I could really feel were the doombeat of his heart and the collapsing walls of his will.

I planned to go on a diet right after the baby was born. But for now I was growing, stretching my skin to translucency, to an iridescent glow.

Howard assured me that he loved me this way, statuesque he called it.

"Petite is going out of style," my mother said.

"Ah, beautiful," Howard murmured in the husky voice of sex, as he burrowed in.

But I'm nobody's fool. On Sundays I saw him look through the magazine section of the *Times* and pause with wistful concentration at those slender models in the brassiere ads.

There is desire beyond mere lust in that, I thought. He might have looked at girls in centerfolds instead, at the opulent ones who were there to inspire a different and simpler kind of longing. If, in his secret heart, he wanted me to be slim and trim, I would be. The women's magazines were full of easy formulas I could follow: The Thinking Woman's Diet, The Drinking Woman's Diet, The Shrinking Woman's Diet. It would be a cinch.

But in the meantime I kept growing while, inside my bulk, the future me stepped daintily, waiting for release.

The baby grew, too, in its confinement, pulsed and sounded its limits.

And Howard was madly in love with it. It was a romance he had never experienced before. He had always had women, of course, and they still sought him out. I watched, narrow-eyed, as new ones came up, threatened, and disappeared. But Howard was inviolate. He was a family man now. And I was the monument to his new life.

"I'm going to diet when this is all over. Become très chic."

"No," he protested. "Don't."

I did a little pirouette. "This stuff is going to fall off like snakeskins."

"Don't lose my favorite parts," Howard warned.

We went to visit other couples who nested in their apartments. Judy and Lenny Miller had a little girl named Roberta. Her toys were always in evidence; a vaporizer was her constant bedside companion.

Howard and I tiptoed in to admire her. When she was awake she was a fresh kid, the kind who screams whenever she speaks, and who answers civil, friendly questions with, "No, silly," or, "No, stupid," a precocious kid who makes nose-picking a public performance.

But now the steam curled her hair into heartbreaking tendrils. The hiss of the vaporizer and the sweet rush of her breath. We whispered in this shrine, made reverent by the miracle.

When we tiptoed back to the living room, I thought, Howard doesn't even feel trapped. He actually wants a baby, wants this whole homely scene for his own. And I hadn't really trapped him anyway, had I? Isn't the sperm the true aggressor, those little Weissmullers breast-stroking to their destiny? Or is the egg the bully, after all, waiting in ambush, ready to mug the first innocent stray?

"Who *really* did this?" I once asked Howard.

But he thought it was a theological poser. "God, I suppose, if you believe in Him," he said.

We sat in the Millers' living room among the debris and leavings of playtime. Howard rested a proprietary hand on my belly. All conversation came back to the inevitable subject.

"My doctor said he never saw anything like it," Judy said. "He had real tears streaming down his face when he held Roberta up."

It might have been sweat, I thought. Motherhood could make some women whitewash anything. She talked about the natural childbirth course they had taken, where she had learned to breathe the right way during labor, so that she was able to be a really active member of the delivery team.

Lenny had been there, too. Now he picked up a bronzed baby shoe and allowed us to observe the wonder of its size in the width of his palm. "It was a beautiful experience," Lenny said. "Most of the time we're working against nature in the births of our children. It's hypocrisy to keep the father outside, a stranger at the gates, so to speak."

What a metaphor!

He advised Howard not to be that notorious slacker, the biological father who drops his seed and runs. Lenny had been right there, rubbing Judy's back, speaking encouragement, talking and stroking his child into the world.

I could sense Howard's excitement.

Then Judy brought out the photographs. We had seen them before, of course, but it seemed appropriate to see them once again, at that moment. Lenny was careful to hand them to us in proper chronological sequence. Judy, huge, horizontal on the delivery table. Himself, the masked robber of innocence, smiling at her with his eyes. The doctor, glistening with sweat/tears, his hand upward and lost to view.

Oh, God, what was I doing?

Judy, grimacing, clenching, contracting, all her agonies reflected in the other faces.

"See?" Lenny pointed out. "I was in labor, too." Then, "Here she comes!" he said, handing us the one with the emerging head, a small, bloodied, and determined ball. Judy's own head was lifted in an effort to watch, and she was smiling.

Then, triumph! The whole family united at last on this shore. Mortal, tender, exquisite. These were winning photos—there was no denying that. Howard was speechless with emotion.

"I thought I was dying, that's all," my mother said. "You were ripping me to shreds."

My father left the room.

"He can't stand to hear about it," my mother whispered. "They feel guilty, you know."

"Howard and I are taking a course," I said.

"A course! What are they going to teach you—how to scream? *You* were feet first," she said accusingly.

But I wasn't put off by her. She had lied about everything else most of my life. "God helps those who help themselves," she used to say. And, "All cats are gray in the dark." That, about lovemaking!

Howard and I went to a class where I learned to breathe. We saw films on the development of the embryo and the benefits of nursing. Howard read aloud from a book on prenatal care, and I took a vitamin supplement that came in pink-and-blue capsules.

I learned to pant, little doglike huffs and puffs for the last stages of labor. I practiced smiling into the bathroom mirror while I panted, in imitation of Judy's radiant Madonna smile of the last photograph.

We had decided against delivery room photographs for ourselves. Everything would be recorded perfectly in the darkroom of the heart.

Howard and I cherished our new vocabulary. *Term.* I was carrying to full *term. Dilation. Presentation. Lactation.* Gorgeous words from a loftier language.

Our lovemaking took on the added excitement of imposed restraint. "Are you all right?" Howard would ask over and over. What a paradox—to be so powerful and fragile at once! Soon we would have to abstain completely for a while and restore our previous virtue.

We played with names for the baby, from the biblical to the historical to the mythical. Nothing seemed good enough or suitably original.

We waited. I went for monthly checkups. Other pregnant women in the doctor's waiting room and I smiled knowingly at one another. We found ourselves in a vast and ancient sorority without the rituals of pledging. Reducing us to girlish dependence, Dr. Marvin Kramer called us by our first names. We called him Dr. Kramer.

Opening my legs on the examining table while his cheerless nurse laid a sheet across my knees for the sake of discretion, I could just make out the crown of his head, halo-lit by his miner's lamp. But I could hear his voice as it tunneled through me. "You're coming along fine, Paulette. Good girl, good girl."

Well, if you can't be good, be careful. That wasn't one of my mother's chestnuts. But it could have been. I had been careless anyway, lost forever to the common sense of practical advice. So many future destinies, irrevocably set. It was astonishing.

"I can hardly move anymore," I complained to Howard one day. He crawled to a corner of the bed and folded himself to give me the most possible room.

The gestation of a brooding elephant is almost two years. Mindless hamsters pop out in sixteen days.

"It will be over soon, Paulie," Howard said, and he reached across the bed and touched my hair.

Then what? I wondered.

"Do the breathing," Howard suggested.

"Take gas when the time comes," my mother said. "Have I ever led you astray?"

Judy and Lenny came to visit with Roberta, who whined and tap-danced on our coffee table.

"I'm going on five hundred calories a day," I said, "as soon as I drop this load."

"Try to sound more maternal," Howard whispered.

"Short skirts are coming back," I said in a threatening voice. "And those skimpy little blouses."

"Oh, just breathe," he begged.

"I'm sick of breathing," I said.

Labor began in the afternoon. It was a dispirited Sunday and we were listening to a melancholy symphony on the radio. Another station, with a Baptist church service, drifted in and out.

The elevator stopped five times for other passengers on the way down to the lobby of our building. Neighbors smiled at us and looked away, pretending they didn't know where we were going with my inflated belly and little overnight case. Inside their pockets they counted on their fingers and were satisfied.

When we came to the hospital, Howard immediately declared to the admitting receptionist that he was a Participating Father and that he was going up with me.

She laughed out loud and continued to type information on the insurance forms.

"It's not too bad so far," I told Howard, wondering why my mother always exaggerated everything.

"I'll be with you," he promised.

They made him wait downstairs despite his protests. "We won't be needing you for a while," the receptionist told him, and she winked at me.

"Good-bye," I said at the elevator. I wished we had decided in favor of pictures, after all. I would have started right there with a record of his poor face as the elevator door closed and the nurse and I went up.

"Primipara!" she shouted to someone I couldn't see, as soon as we left the elevator.

Well, that sounds nice, I thought. Like prima donna or prima ballerina. We went swiftly down a corridor, past little rooms. Other women looked out at me.

What's all this? I wondered, everything unlearned in that first bolt of fear.

I had my own room. A Room of One's Own, I thought bitterly. But I climbed into the high bed anyway, like a drowsy and obedient child.

The new doctors who came to examine me all seemed so short. And they smiled as they dug in and announced their findings. "Two fingers," they said. "Three fingers."

Why didn't they use some medical jargon for what they were doing? It sounded suspiciously like juvenile sex play to me, as if they were only *playing* doctor.

It was such a quiet place. There was none of my mother's famous screaming. Things must have changed, I decided, since her day.

After a while I was shaved, for collaborating with the enemy, I supposed. More silence. Then a shriek! I sat up, alerted, but it was only some horseplay among the nurses. "What's going on?" I asked someone who came in and went out again without answering. "Hello?"

It was lonely. Where was Howard, anyway?

And then he was there. When had he grown that shad-owed jowl? And why were his eyes so dark with sympathy?

"It's nothing," I said severely. "Stop looking like that."

Lenny had seemed so splendorous. Howard only looked mournful and terrified. So this was where his life had led him.

Things didn't get better. Howard rubbed my back and jerked me from the haven of short dozes with his murmurs, his restless movement. There were noises now from other rooms as well. Voices rose in wails of protest.

But I had my own troubles. The contractions were coming so damn fast. I was thirsty, but water wasn't permitted—only the rough swipe of a washcloth across my tongue. I caught it with my teeth and tried to suck on it, cheating.

There was no discreet examination sheet in this place. Strangers peered at me in full view. They measured, probed, and went away. A nurse sneaked a hypodermic into my thigh when I wasn't looking.

"Hey, what's that?" I demanded. "I'm not supposed to have anything. This is a *natural* case, you know."

"Dr. Kramer is on his way," she said, evading the issue.

"Taking his own sweet time," I snarled.

Howard seemed shocked by my rudeness and by the abrupt shift of mood.

"This is getting *bad*," I told him. But it wasn't what he wanted to hear.

They wheeled me at breakneck speed to the delivery room. Howard ran alongside, a winded trainer trying to keep up with his fighter. "Almost there," he gasped.

How would *he* know? It was miles and miles.

Despite everything, they strapped me down. "This is barbaric!" I shouted. "Women on farms used to squat in the fields!"

"Oh, God, *that* bullshit again," a nurse said.

"You trapped me into this," I told Howard. "I'll never forgive you. Never!"

He was wearing a green surgical mask and now he stood as poised and eager as an outfielder waiting for the long ball.

"Impostor!" I cried.

"Paulette!" Dr. Kramer called. "How is my big girl?"

"Just tell me what to do," Howard said.

"You've already done your part, pal," Dr. Kramer told him. "Now just hold her hand."

I yowled and Howard said, "My love, I'm here!" His eyes were brilliant with tears.

The whole room shuddered with pain. And I was the center of it, the spotlit star of the universe. Who was trying to be born here, anyway, Moby Dick?

Oh, all the good, wise things I had done in my life.

I might have done anything and still come to this.

In school the teacher rolled down charts on nutrition. We saw the protein groups, the grain groups. Green leafy vegetables. Lack of vitamin C leads to scurvy.

Liars! The charts ought to show this, the extraordinary violence of this, worse than mob violence, worse than murder. FUCKING LEADS TO THIS! those charts ought to say.

"A few more pushes and you'll have your baby," Dr. Kramer said.

Ah, who wanted a baby? For once in her whole rotten life, my mother was right. "Dr. Kramer! Marvin! Give me gas!" I screamed.

But instead he caught the baby, who had shouldered through in the excitement.

And I had forgotten to smile. I had greeted my child with the face of a madwoman.

Somewhere else in the room a nurse pressed Howard's head down between his knees.

"No pictures. No pictures," I said.

(1976)

Mrs. X

I am bigger than life. Everything—my hands, feet—a stand-in for the Russian Women's Decathlon champ, a thing of beauty and power. Everyone is big nowadays, my mother says—*her* hands and feet like tiny blunt instruments. She used to give me five lamb chops for dinner, scattering the peas and carrots to create an illusion. Everyone eats more nowadays, she sighs. But the spoon chimes against her teeth as she drops her dollop of cottage cheese.

But say, listen, there is more to me than meets the eye, more than is seen on the wide screen. More than the breasts weighting their hammock or the great head ducking in doorways. Underneath there is a domestic heart with the modest beat of a ladies' wristwatch. My dreams are so simple they could be laid out on a kitchen table for examination. I stand here at the window behind the coy and frilly curtains in this building in a terrible complex of buildings. I watch as my family take their places in the playground. There is the boy Jason, a rosy nucleus in the sandbox. There are Howard and baby Ann, moving in serene rhythm as he pushes her in a swing. They adorn the playground like three brave flags in bright sweaters I've knitted for them. I become excited with pride as if I had knitted *them* and not just their sweaters.

Deep in the pocket of my apron is the letter from an anonymous friend.

> *My dear,* [she advises]
> *Watch out for Howard and Mrs. X of B building. You know what I mean. Although I am not what you would refer to as a devout person, I will pray for you anyway.*
>
> *Your Anonymous Friend*

Thanks a lot. Wasn't everything perfect before? Now I must be guarded, breathe softly so as not to miss the innuendos. If Howard volunteers to help with the laundry? If he compares my bleach to hers near the double-duty dryers? Never fear. The management has installed klieg lights at the request of the tenants who wear tight capri pants. Nothing clandestine in the laundry room.

Oh, get lost, my loyal anonymous friend! You've upset the order of my life, scattered the importance of my values. Who cares now if the sirloin-tip roast is well-marbled? Who wants the PTA to take a firm stand on intramurals?

Big as I am I can't lurk in doorways and narrow passages to catch them out.

But what if I don't wait and watch but simply lift the window now and jump, waft slowly toward him, eighteen stories, eighteen neighbors to wave to in descent. My mother would shout to me in comfort, Everyone is dying nowadays!

There he is, my Howard, the best father in the world. Protective as a mother hen. (Jason sits on his lap at the dentist's so that the father can absorb the pain of the child.)

I open the window and look down. Howard in the green sweater is standing alone. Both children are together in the sandbox. Cutting across the playground, as if on choreographic cue, comes the woman in the red coat. She is wearing boots of course and they zigzag in neat steps until she is near him. Her hair is long, that much I can see; nothing more without tumbling out.

Wait, I shout, don't do anything, and I run to the children's room and look through the chaos of the toy box until I find them, those binoculars that their *other* grandfather, that cheap voyeur, bought for Jason. Wait, wait! I call again, and when I go to the window and bring them into focus, they are standing there and her foot is pointed outward as if she is threatening to go. Howard's hands are in his pockets, where they belong. They are haloed together in the rainbow nimbus of the rotten binoculars. Her hand touches his arm, but I can't see his face.

Mrs. X, I say, go away. Leave town. Everything was hunky-dory. What can you know about someone else's marriage? The sloppy intimacy of it. Can you pit "fashionable and lean" against "ample and familiar"? Could boots and false eyelashes win out over this apron? Purple lilies on a blue field. You wouldn't have a chance. We only need an extra bedroom, and we're on the management's list for a five, with terrace.

Don't complicate my life, I shout, and the woman on the twentieth floor shakes out her mop and dust-curl stars fall on my head.

He moves and places his hand on her waist. Gracefully (I'll give her that), she turns her head and lowers her chin; one might guess that they are going to dance a tango. Slow, slow, quick, quick. Begin! One, two, and she breaks away from him.

Run, run, I yell. He isn't worth it. I'm going to kill him anyway. I'm going to kill him in the place you both go—if I only knew where it is. The community basement room is just for New Year's parties and Girl Scout meetings and Civil Defense. The Tenants' Committee would never approve of *that*. So where do you go and why do you go, and looking through the binoculars I see him catch up, and linking arms they disappear at the concrete corner of Building C.

Murderer! I yell. Help, police, and my voice goes up like a helium balloon. The children are left alone in the Sinai Desert of the sandbox, in this mad city.

It isn't fair because it shouldn't be me so big and wounded on the receiving end. Listen, I made compromises when I saw him for the first time in all his rumpled charm. And I let it pass when he saw me and said all those needless things about white valleys and Rubens when a simple "ooh" would have been just right.

Then I look again and here he comes, my Howard, like a victor from battle, and I have to give him credit, he goes right to the children.

So that's how it is, and I let the elevator make its silent climb, nineteen stories, while I rub my hands together and make plans.

But then he comes through the doorway with his beautiful and powerful weapons: the baby Ann collapsed on his shoulder, her overall leg pulled up over a chapped knee; Jason with a blood-freezing hold on his father's leg. And he himself with ruddy cheeks from the outdoors, in a green sweater, in trousers. The idiot eyes of the binoculars bang against my breast.

Howard lets me look at a pained profile and I wait. For a moment I think: here is the evidence around my neck like a weighty chain, as if the binoculars had captured forever that action, that blurred vision, and I could have *shown* him what I saw.

Howard taps his finger on the Formica counter. "I have to quit smoking," he says.

"What?"

"I have to quit smoking. There's no kidding myself. It's killing me. I can't run one block."

"Why don't you just cut down?"

"Because that's horseshit. But the minute I think about giving it up, I change my mind. I don't want to do it."

"You can do it, Howard."

"Ah, who wants to? You have to die from something anyway."

"Listen. You can do it, Howard. I'll buy you lots of stuff to chew on, stuff you haven't had in years, like Black Jack gum and Jujubes."

"Yeah?" He is dreamy but interested.

Jason pulls away from his father and comes to me. "Mommy," he says. "My mommy." He pats my arm.

"Howard, you can give up smoking!" I think I'm shouting. I can't help it, like a fool I feel so happy.

"Well, maybe," he concedes. "With God's help," he adds, because he is cautious.

"*I'll* help you," I cry. "I'll even go on a diet."

Howard looks at me for the first time. He smiles. "You don't have to do that."

"No, no, I want to. It's the least I can do."

I am thrilled with the idea of a joint effort. It is like the camaraderie at a block party in the Bronx on V-J Day. The war is over. We are going to live forever.

I wonder, do I know anybody with a Xerox machine? I will make a thousand copies of a letter to my anonymous friend.

Dear Friend,
What my husband does is his business, and I'll kill you if
you tell lies about him and spread rumors.

I'll stick a copy in every mail slot in every building in the complex.

Howard stands and leans against the refrigerator. I lift the binoculars to my eyes thinking I am due for a miracle, a vision, but I see only him, his edges soft pink, yellow, and orange, and the words "frost free" near his left ear.

(1969)

Sundays

Howard is the beauty in this family. Even the mirrors in our apartment are hung at his eye level. I don't mind. What's wrong with a little role reversal, anyway? What's so bad about a male sex object, for a change? That ability to sprout hair like dark fountains, the flat tapering planes of his buttocks and hips, and oh, those *hands*, and erections pointing the way to bed like road markers.

Besides, I have my own good points, not the least of them my disposition. Sunny, radiant, I wake with the same dumb abundance of hope every day. The bed always seems too small to contain both me and that expansion of joy.

It's only Thursday or Sunday. It's only my own flesh, smelling like bread near my rooting nose. Nothing special has happened, for which I am grateful. Anything might happen, for which I am expectant and tremblingly ready.

On the other hand, Howard is depressed, hiding in the sheets, moaning in his dream. Even without opening my eyes, I can feel the shape of his mood beside me. Then my eyes do open. Ta-da! Another gorgeous day! Just what I expected. The clock hums, electric, containing its impulse to tick, the wallpaper repeats itself around the room, and Howard buries his face in his pillow, refusing to come to terms with the dangers of consciousness.

My hand is as warm and as heavy as a baby's head, and I lay it against his neck, palm up. If I let him sleep, he would do it for hours and hours. That's depression.

Years ago, my mother woke me with a song about a bird on a windowsill and about sunshine and flowers and the glorious feeling of being alive that had nothing in the world to do with the sad still life of a school lunch and the reluctant walk in brown oxfords, one foot and then the other, for six blocks. It had nothing to do with that waxed ballroom of a gymnasium and the terrible voice of the whistle that demanded agility and grace where there were only clumsy confusion and an enormous desire to be the other girl on the other team, the one leaping in memory toward baskets and dangling ropes.

I didn't want to get up, either—at least not until I had grown out of it, grown away from teachers, grown out of that thin body in an undershirt and lisle stockings and garter belt abrasive on sharp hipbones. I would get up when I was good and ready, when it was all over and I could have large breasts and easy friendships.

Howard blames his depression on real things in his real life because he doesn't believe in the unconscious. At parties where all the believers talk about the interpretation of dreams, about wish fulfillment and surrogate symbols, Howard covers his mouth with one hand and mutters, "What crap!"

Is he depressed because his parents didn't want him to be born, because his mother actually hoisted his father in her arms every morning for a month, hoping to bring on that elusive period? Not a chance!

Is he sad because his sister was smarter in school, or at least more successful, or because she talked him into stealing a dollar from their mother's purse and then squealed? Never!

He is depressed, he says, because it starts to rain when he's at a ball game and the men pulling the tarpaulin over the infield seem to be covering a mass grave. He is sad, he says, because his boss is a prick and the kid living upstairs roller-skates in the kitchen.

Ah, Howard. My hand is awake now, buzzing with blood, and it kneads the flesh of his neck and then his back, works down through the warm tunnel of bedclothes until it finds his hand and squeezes hard. "It's a fabulous day, lover! Hey, kiddo, wake up and I'll tell you something."

Howard opens his eyes, but they are glazed and without focus. "Huh?"

"Do you know what?" Searching my head for therapeutic news.

His vision finds the room, the morning light, his whole life. His eyes close again.

"Howard. It's Sunday, the day of rest. The paper is outside, thick and juicy, hot off the press. I'll make waffles and sausages for breakfast. Do you want to go for a drive in the country?"

"Oh, for Christ's sake, will you leave me alone! I want to sleep."

"Sleep? Sweetheart, you'll sleep enough when you're dead."

I see that idea roll behind his eyelids. Death. What next?

The children whisper like lovers in the other bedroom.

"Come on, sleepyhead, get up. We'll visit model homes. We'll look in the paper for some new ones." I pat him on the buttocks, a loving but fraternal gesture, a manager sending his favorite man into the game.

Why am I so happy? It must be the triumph of the human spirit over genetics and environment. I know the same bad things Howard knows. I have my ups and downs, traumas, ecstasies. Maybe this happiness is only a dirty trick, another of life's big come-ons. I might end up the kind who can't ride on escalators or sit in chairs that don't have arms. Who knows?

But in the meantime I sing as I whip up waffle batter, while Howard drops pages of the *Times* like leaves from a deciduous tree.

I sing songs from the forties, thinking there's nothing in this life like your own nostalgia. I sing "Hut-Sut

Rawlson on the Riller-ah." I sing "Life is like a mardi-gras, funiculi funicula!" The waffles stick to the iron. "Don't sit under the apple tree with anyone else but me," I warn Howard, willing the waffle and coffee smells into the living room where he sits like an inmate in the wintry garden of a small sanatorium.

"*Breakfast is ready!*" I have the healthy bellow of a short-order cook.

He shuffles in, still convalescing from his childhood.

The children come in, too, his jewels, his treasures. Daddy! They climb his legs to reach the table, to scratch themselves on his morning beard, and he runs his hands over them, a blind man trying to memorize their bones. The teakettle sings, the sun crashes in through the window, and my heart will not be swindled.

"What's the matter, Howie? If something is bothering you, talk about it."

He smiles, that calculated half-smile, and I think that we hardly talk about anything that matters.

I waited all my life to become a woman, damn it, to sit in a kitchen and say grown-up things to the man facing me, words that would float like vapor over the heads of the children. Don't I remember that language from my own green days, code words in Yiddish and pig Latin, and a secret but clearly sexual jargon that made my mother laugh and filled me with a dark and turbulent longing and rage?

Ix-nay, the *id*-kay.

Now I want to talk over the heads of *my* children, in the modern language of the cinema. There are thousands of words they wouldn't understand and would never remember, except for the rhythm and the mystery.

Fellatio, Howard. *Vasectomy*.

He rattles the Real Estate section and slowly turns the pages.

"Well, did you find a development for us? Find one with a really inspired name this time."

I try so hard to encourage him. Looking at model homes has become a standard treatment for Howard's depression. For some reason we believe the long drive out of the city, the ordered march through unlived-in rooms, restores him. Not that *we* want to live in the suburbs. How we laugh and poke one another at the roped-off bedrooms hung in velvet drapery, the rubber chickens roosting in warm refrigerators. The thing is, places like that confirm our belief in our own choices. We're *safe* here in the city, in our tower among towers. Flyspecks, so to speak, in the population.

On other days, we've gone to Crestwood Estates, Seaside Manor (miles from any sea), to Tall Oaks and Sweet Pines, to *Châteaux Printemps*, and Chalets-on-the-Sound.

But the pickings are slim now. All the worthwhile land has been gobbled up by speculators, and those tall oaks and sweet pines fallen to bulldozers. There are hardly any developments left for our sad Sundays. The smart money is in garden apartments and condominiums, cities without skylines. Maybe later, when we are older, we'll visit the Happy Haven and the Golden Years Retreat, to purge whatever comes with mortality and the final vision.

But now Howard is trying. "Here's one," he says. "*Doncastle Greens. Only fifty minutes from the heart of Manhattan. Live like a king on a commoner's budget.*"

"Let me see!" I rush to his side, ready for conspiracy. "Hey, listen to this. *Come on down today and choose either a twenty-one-inch color TV or a deluxe dishwasher, as a bonus, absolutely free!* Howie, what do you choose?"

But Howard chooses silence, will not be cajoled so easily, so early in his depression.

I hide the dishes under a veil of suds and we all get dressed. The children are too young to care where we are going, as long as they can ride in the car, the baby steering crazily in her car seat and Jason contemplating the landscape and the faces of other small boys poised at the windows of other cars.

The car radio sputters news and music and frantic advice. It is understood that Howard will drive there and I will drive back.

He sits forward, bent over the wheel, as if visibility is poor and the traffic hazardous. In fact, it's a marvelous, clear day and the traffic is moving without hesitation past all the exits; past the green signs and the abandoned wrecks like modern sculpture at roadside; past dead dogs, their brilliant innards squeezed out onto the divider.

Jason points, always astounded at the first corpse, but we are past it before he can speak. It occurs to me that everywhere here there are families holding dangling leashes and collars, walking through the yards of their neighborhoods, calling, "Lucky! Lucky!" and then listening for that answering bark that will never come. Poor Lucky, deader than a doornail, flatter than a bath mat.

I watch Howard, that elegant nose so often seen in profile, that wavy hoodlum's hair, and his ear, unspeakably vulnerable, waxen and convoluted.

And then we are there. Doncastle Greens is a new one for us. The builder obviously dreamed of moats and grazing sheep. Model No. I, the Shropshire, recalls at once gloomy castles and thatched cottages, Richard III and Miss Marple. Other cars are already parked under the colored banners when we pull in.

The first step is always the brochure, wonderfully new and smelly with printer's ink. The motif is British, of course, and there are taprooms and libraries as opposed to the dens and funrooms of Crestwood Estates, *les salons et les chambres de Châteaux Printemps.*

Quelle savvy!

The builder's agent is young and balding, busy sticking little flags into promised lots on a huge map behind his desk. He calls us folks. "Good to see you, folks!" Every once in a while he rubs his hands together as if selling homes makes one cold. During his spiel I try to catch Howard's eye, but Howard pretends to be listening. What an actor!

We move in a slow line through Model I, behind an elderly couple. I know we've seen them before, at Tall Oaks perhaps, but there are no greetings exchanged. They'll never buy, of course, and I wonder about their motives, which are probably more devious than ours.

Some of the people, I can see, are really buyers. One wife holds her husband's hand as if they are entering consecrated premises.

I poke Howard, just below the heart, a bully's semaphore. I can talk without moving my lips. "White brocade couch on bowlegs," I mutter. "Definitely velvet carpeting." I wait, but Howard is grudging.

"Plastic-covered lampshades," he offers, finally.

I urge him on. "Crossed rifles over the fireplace. Thriving fake dracaena in the entrance." I snicker, roll my eyes, do a little soft-shoe.

But Howard isn't playing. He is leaning against the braided ropes that keep us from muddying the floor of the drawing room, and he looks like a man at the prow of a ship.

"Howard?" Tentative. Nervous.

"You know, kiddo, it's not really that bad," he says.

"Do you mean the *house*?"

Howard doesn't answer. The older man takes a tape measure from his pocket and lays it against the dark molding. Then he writes something into a little black notebook.

The buyers breathe on our necks, staring at their future. "Oh, *Ronnie*," she says, an exhalation like the first chords of a hymn. I would not be surprised if she kneels now or makes some other religious gesture.

"One of these days," Howard says, "*pow*, one of us will be knocked on the head in that crazy city. Raped. Strangled."

"Howie . . ."

"And do we have adequate bookshelves? You know I have no room for my books."

The oak bookshelves before us hold all the volumes, A through Z, of the *American Household Encyclopedia*.

The old man measures the doorframe and writes again in his book. Perhaps he will turn around soon and measure us, recording his findings in a feathery hand.

Jason and another boy discover each other and stare like mirrors. What would happen if we took the wrong one home, bathed him and gave him Frosted Flakes, kissed him and left the night-light on until he forgot everything else and adjusted? The baby draws on her pacifier and dreamily pets my hair.

Everyone else has passed us and Howard is still in the same doorway. I pull on his sleeve. "The baby is getting heavy."

He takes her from me and she nuzzles his cheek with her perfect head.

We proceed slowly to the master bathroom, the one with the dual vanities and a magazine rack embossed with a Colonial eagle.

"Howie, will you look at this. *His and hers.*"

He doesn't answer.

We go into the bedroom itself, where ghosts of dead queens rest on the carved bed. "Mortgages. Cesspools. Community living." I face him across the bed and hiss the words at him, but he doesn't even wince. He looks sleepy and relaxed. I walk around the bed and put my arm through his. "Maybe we ought to join Marriage Encounter, after all. Maybe we look in the wrong places for our happiness, Howard."

He pats my hand, solicitous but distracted. I walk behind him now, a tourist following a guide. At ye olde breakfast nooke, I want to sit him down and explain that I am terrified of change, that the city is my hideout and my freedom, that one of us might take a lover, or worse.

But I am silent in the pantry, in the wine cellar and the vestibule, and we are finished with the tour of the house, evicted before occupation. We stand under the fluttering banners and watch the serious buyers reenter the builder's trailer. Howard shifts the baby from arm to arm as if she interferes with his concentration. Finally, he passes her to me without speaking. He puts his hands into his pockets and he has that dreaming look on his face.

"*I'll* drive back," I say, as if this weren't preordained.

There is more traffic now, and halfway home we slow to observe the remains of an accident. Some car has jumped the guardrail and there is a fine icing of shattered glass on the road.

"Do you *see*?" I say, not sure of my meaning.

But Howard is asleep, his head tilted against the headrest. At home, I can see that he's coming out of it. He is interested in dinner, in the children's bath. He stands behind me at the sink and he has an erection.

Later, in bed again, I get on top, for the artificial respiration I must give. His mouth opens to receive my tongue, a communion wafer. I rise above him, astonished by the luminosity of my skin in the half-light.

Howard smiles up at me, suffused with pleasure, yes, with *happiness*, his ghosts mugged and banished from this room.

"Are you happy?" I must know, restorer of faith, giver of life. "Are you happy?"

And even as I wait for his answer, my own ghosts enter, stand solemn at the foot of the bed, thin girls in undershirts, jealous and watchful, whispering in some grown-up language I can never understand.

(1974)

Nights

What men must learn is that there are some women in this world who are never satisfied, who move through their homes with the restlessness of dayworkers. Even their blood seems restless, rising and falling so that they are alternately pale or flushed, and suffer from dizzy spells and capricious moods. I am one of these women.

Sometimes Howard will ask, "What's the *matter* with you?" or "What do you want?" But he knows that these are only mind mutterings. I want nothing. I want everything. I am given to looking through windows like a sentinel, fumbling through the mail as if for secret messages, picking up the telephone with renewed expectancy.

Hello, hello—but it is always someone I know.

Staring out through the bedroom window in the middle of the night, I wish that everyone else in the complex would wake, too, that lights would go on with the easy magic of stars in a Disney sky. I look at Howard, who is asleep, and I can see his eyes moving under those thin lids as he follows his dreams. I lean toward him, look more closely, and see his nostrils flare with his breath.

"Howard? Howard, I can't sleep."

He sighs deeply and his hands open at his sides as if in supplication, but he continues to sleep.

In the next room, the children are asleep.

Across the city, my mother and father sleep on high twin beds, like sister and brother. There is always a night-light, as decorous as a firefly, burning in their hallway, so that my father can find his way to the bathroom. There is a picture of me on the dresser in their bedroom, and another of the children. My father sleeps with his socks on, even in the summer. My mother keeps a handkerchief tied to the strap of her nightgown.

Do they dream of each other?

Does Howard dream of me?

If I ever sleep, I will have baroque dreams that would have challenged Freud, dreams that could be sold to the movies.

But I cannot sleep.

On other nights Howard pulls himself awake for a moment, glares at the clock, at my bedside light, at the pile of magazines, suitable for an invalid, balanced on my chest. "For God's sake, go to sleep," he hisses, as if it were a matter of choice.

Once I complained to my mother about my insomnia. She is old-fashioned and believes in remedies. "Drink milk," she urged. "Do calisthenics. Open the window."

My father, who likes to get a word in edgewise, said, "Forgetting."

We never questioned his meaning.

But I am here alone in this stillness in which I have a dog's sense of hearing, can hear beds creak, distant telephones, letters whispering down mail slots on every floor.

Who writes letters at this hour? Who is calling?

The dead eye of the television set faces me. If I turn it on, I will find old movie stars carrying on business as usual, stranded forever in time with their hairstyles and clothes. There will be a comedy and I will laugh, taking deep breaths. I will grow sleepy, child-sleepy, milk-warm and drifting, with arms heavy and legs that pull me down. Maybe there will be news, even at this hour. Isn't it daytime in China, midnight in California? Surely there will be bad news and the ominous voice of the commentator to intone it. Ladies and gentlemen, here is some bad news that has just come in . . . Howard will wake, the children will cry out in their sleep, the old lady downstairs will bang on her ceiling with a broom.

I walk to the window again and there *are* other lights on in the complex—two or three.

At parties we go to, everyone complains of being an insomniac. Women insist they haven't slept in years. One man walks the room repeating, "Three hours, *three hours*," to anyone who will listen. He has a built-in alarm that never allows him to sleep a minute longer. That's too bad, say the women who never sleep, but they are insincere. Another man suggests it is guilt that won't let us sleep, but the women unite against him. Guilt? The truly guilty sleep to escape their guilt. Ask the ones with old mothers in nursing homes. Ask the ones whose children wet the beds, the ones whose husbands are listless or lonely. Someone changes the subject. We refill glasses.

It is not even too hot to sleep. It is a perfect summer night, with a breeze rushing in through the screens. The sheets aren't sticky and hot.

Howard is sprawled in wonderful sleep.

I sit on the floor and place myself in the half-lotus position and clasp my hands behind my head. I draw my breath in deeply and then slowly let it out, lowering my right elbow to the floor. Then the left elbow. There is a carpet smell as I lower my head. It is not unpleasant. I look under the bed and see one of the children's shoes lying on its side. I crawl there to get it and then I lie on my back, watching the changes in the box spring as Howard shifts his weight. From my position under the bed, I can see under the dresser and the night tables, where there are glints of paper clips and other lost and silvery things. There is a photograph that has fallen from the frame of the large mirror, and I crawl across the floor and reach for it. It is a picture of a group of friends at a party. We are all holding cocktail glasses and cigarettes. The women are sitting upright to make their breasts seem larger, and one of the men has his hand across his wife's behind.

We are all going to grow old. The men will have heart attacks, the women will lose the loyalty of tissue in chins and breasts.

I want to go to the mirror and raise my nightgown and look at myself for reassurance. But I walk into the children's room instead. Jason sleeps well and is a handsome child, and yet I am filled with sorrow at the sight of him. I see that it is all false—the posters of astronauts, the books to teach him of birds and fishes and flowers. The baby is in her crib, legs and arms opened as if sleep were a lover she welcomes. The Japanese mobile trembles a warning, and I tiptoe out and go into the kitchen.

I choose soft, quiet foods that will not disturb the silence: raisins, cheese, marshmallows. I put the last marshmallow on the end of a fork and toast it over the gas range.

I do not believe it, but I tell myself that I will be able to sleep with a full stomach. I take my mother's advice and drink a glass of milk.

If I had a dog, if we were allowed to keep pets in the complex, the dog might be a companion when I cannot sleep. I had a dog when I was a child. When it was a few years old, I realized with horror I had established an irrevocable relationship that could only end in death. From this grew the knowledge that death was true of all relationships—friendships, marriage. I began to treat the dog indifferently, even cruelly sometimes, pushing him away when he jumped up to greet me. But it didn't matter. The dog died and I mourned him anyway. For a long time I kept his dish and a gnawed rubber bone.

I suppose a dog awakened in the middle of the night would not understand. He would probably want to eat and be taken for a walk. And of course Howard is allergic to animal hair. We have a bowl of goldfish in the kitchen. There are two, one with beautiful silver overtones to his scales. There is a plant in their bowl and colored pebbles at the bottom. The fish swim as if they had a destination, around and around and around.

I shut the kitchen light and go back into the bedroom. I yawn twice, thinking, well, that's a good sign. Sleep can't be very far away and the main thing is not to panic. I climb into bed and Howard rolls away to his side.

God, it's the silence, the large silence and the small, distant sounds. If I could talk, even shout, I might feel better. "I can't sleep and life stinks on ice," I whisper. Silence. I raise my voice slightly. "I can't sleep and tomorrow, *today*, I won't be able to stand anything." Silence. "Howard, my mother and father didn't want me to marry you. My mother said that you have bedroom eyes. My father said that you were not ambitious."

A song I have not heard in years comes into my head. First I mouth the words. Then I try to whisper the tune. But my voice is throaty and full.

"Shhhh," Howard warns in his sleep.

Oh, think, think. Come up with something else. But the song is stuck there. Doo-bee doo dee-dee, a song I never really liked. I try to overwhelm it with something symphonic. So this is what I've come to, I think, and the song leaves my head, like a bird from a tree. Instantly other birds flock in: shopping lists, the 20/20 line on the eye chart, a chain letter to which I never responded. Do not break the chain or evil will befall your house. Continue it and long life and good health will be yours to enjoy and cherish. In eight weeks you will receive 1,120 picture postcards from all over the world.

Will I?

Learned men wear copper bracelets. My mother weeps over broken mirrors. Hearts are broken, bones. They crack in the silence of the night.

Somewhere, in Chicago or St. Louis or Silver Springs, my old lover sleeps on his own side of a king-sized bed. He talks in his sleep and his wife promptly wakes, thin-lipped, alert. In a careful whisper, she questions him. "Who?" she asks. "When? Where?" My lover mumbles something she cannot make out. She plucks gently at the hair on his chest, in shrewd imitation of my style. "Who?" she asks again.

In Howard's dream he is in the war again. His eyes roll frantically and his legs brace against the sheets.

I whisper, "We're pulling out now, men."

His head swivels.

"For Christ's sake, keep down."

His hands grope at his side, sling a rifle.

"Aaargh," I say. "They got me. Die, you bastards!"

The bed shakes with his terror.

"Shh," I say. "It's only a dream. Only a dream."

But he'll die anyway. In this bed, perhaps.

Howard in a coffin. Howard in the earth. Good-bye, Howard.

He sighs, resigned.

I walk to the foot of the bed and stand in a narrow bar of moonlight. My white nightgown is silver and my arms glow as if they were wet. "Look at this, Howard," and I grasp the hem of my gown and twirl it around my body. Then I lift myself onto the balls of my feet and turn slowly, catching my reflection in the mirror, spectral, lovely.

I dip, arch and move across the floor in a silent, voluptuous ballet. "Hey, get a load of this," and I do something marvelously intricate, unlearned. My feet move like small animals. Wow, I think, and Howard flings himself onto his stomach in despair.

I am breathing hard now and I sit in the rocking chair and think of my lover again. His wife has given up the inquisition, but now she can't sleep, either. She goes to the window in Chicago or Silver Springs and gazes sullenly at her property, at her pin oaks and her hemlock, at the children's swings hung in moonlight, at telephone wire stretched into infinity. She pats the curlers on her head and goes into the next room to look at her children.

Across town, my father walks to the bathroom. "What's the matter?" my mother asks.

"Nothing. What do you think?"

Before he comes back to bed, she is plunged into sleep again.

Howard, Howard, Howard. Prices are going up. The house is on fire. My lover is dying of something awful.

My lover is dying, his wife at his side. She is wearing a hat and a coat with a fox collar. She leans over him. "Who?" she persists, and her fierce breath makes the oxygen tent flutter like Saran Wrap.

"Howard. My lover is dying in St. Louis or Chicago. No one really cares, Howard."

Real tears fill my eyes and then roll down my cheeks.

I climb into bed again. If I had a hobby, something to take my mind away. A dog.

I yawn, lowering myself carefully to the pillow. Ah, almost there, almost there, I tell myself in encouragement. One minute you're awake and the next you're in dreamland.

I shut my eyes.

That's right. Shut your eyes. Here comes the Sandman. Here comes dream dust. Here comes.

My eyes are shut tight. My hands are clenched.

I hear something. There is a noise somewhere in the apartment. Maybe I am asleep and only dreaming noise. Maybe I hear the goldfish splashing in their bowl. My eyes open.

What's that? What's that?

Oh, God.

The whole damn world sleeps like a baby—the super-intendent of our building, the new people on the tenth floor, old boyfriends and their wives, their mothers and fathers, their babies, their dogs. Everyone sleeps.

All of the bastards at those parties are liars. They sleep, too, cunningly, maybe with their eyes open, for all I know. They dissolve, they give in, they go under—into the blue and perfect wonder of sleep.

I am the only one here. I am the only one left in the dark world, the only one who cares enough to stay awake the long and awful night.

(1974)

Overtime

Howard's first wife wouldn't let him go. Her hold on him wasn't even sexual—I could have dealt with that. It would have been an all-out war and of course I would have won. There is something final about me, and steadying.

I wondered why he was attracted to her in the first place. It could only have been her pathos. Reenie is little and thin, with large light freckles everywhere. Her bones used to stab him during the night and he couldn't sleep. Howard says I am the first woman he can really *sleep* with, in the literal sense of the word. When he loves me, he says that he feels as if he is embracing the universe, that a big woman is essential to his survival. He feeds me tidbits from his plate at dinner, to support my image and keep up my strength.

Reenie called up night and day. She left cryptic messages for Howard. She even left messages with

Jason, who was only three or four at the time. Jason called her Weeny, insinuating her further into our lives with that nickname. "Weeny needs ten," he would tell me.

We gave Reenie plenty of money, although she denied all legal rights to alimony. They were only married seven months and she decided she didn't *deserve* alimony after such a short relationship, that you can't even collect unemployment insurance unless you've been on the job for a while. But we were always giving her money anyway—ten here, five there. Ostensibly, they were loans, but Reenie was hard-pressed to repay them.

I suggested to Howard that we adopt her, that it would be cheaper, taxwise and all, but Howard seemed to really consider the idea, getting that contemplative look in his eye, chewing his dinner in a slow, even rhythm. I imagined Reenie living with us, another bed in the converted dinette where the children sleep.

I knew intuitively when Reenie was calling. The telephone had a certain insistence to its ring, as if she were willing me to answer it. She wanted to know if Howard remembered a book she used to have, something she was very sentimental about. Could he possibly have taken it by mistake when they split up? Would I just take a look on the shelf while she held on, it has a blue cover. She called to say that she had swollen glands, that she'd been very tired lately and in fluorescent light she could see right through to her bones.

We sent her ten dollars for the doctor. We sent her five for a new book.

At night, when the children were in bed, talcum-sweet and overkissed, Howard and I staggered into the living room to talk. This was the best time of the day. We couldn't afford real analysis, so we did each other instead. I was quite classical in my approach: I went back to my childhood, digging up traumas, but Howard liked to deal with the recent past. He took his old life out like a stamp collection and we looked at it together. Howard talked about his first marriage as if he were just begun then himself, and as if he expected me to feel some regret for the poverty of their relationship. I did. I saw them in their marriage bed, ill-fitting like two parts of different jigsaw puzzles. I listened to Reenie talk him out of sleep, pry him from his dreams with the wrench of her voice. "Is this mole getting darker? Listen, Howard, is this a *lump*?"

She was always a hypochondriac, and Howard began to be one, too. By the time I met him, he was dying from a thousand diseases. I laughed at all of them.

"Are you kidding?" I said.

He was petulant, but hopeful. "How do you know? *You're* not a doctor."

But I wouldn't allow him a single internal mystery, and he was cured. The laying on of hands, I called it, covering him with my own healing flesh. "Oh, you don't know!"

he cried, but I did, and he was cured of palpitations, bruises, nosebleeds, fears of castration.

Yet Reenie stayed on, a dubious legacy. One morning Jason answered the telephone. "Weeny," he said, narrowing his eyes, waiting for my reaction.

I wouldn't give him the satisfaction. "Oh?" I said it coolly, raising my eyebrows. "What does *she* want?"

She wanted to stay with us for a few days. Some madman was after her. A guy she met at Unemployment, a real psycho.

"I'll have to speak to Howard about it," I told her, but that wasn't true.

Jason and I watched a kids' television program where they demonstrated how to make a Chinese lantern out of newspaper. We tried to make one, following the easy directions, but it fell apart. I decided to speak to Jason instead. "Reenie wants to stay here for a few days."

He labored over the lantern, his fingers stiff with paste. "In my bed?"

"Of course not. On the sofa, in the living room. What do you think?"

"I hate this stupid lantern!" he cried, ripping it apart.

The baby was standing in her crib, toes splayed, rattling the bars. "Guess what? Reenie is coming," I told her, despising my own theatrics.

That night I gave the news to Howard, carefully, as if I believed it might be fatal. He sighed, but I knew he was secretly pleased. He wanted to know how long she would stay, what time she would need the bathroom in the morning, and if I could possibly make some tapioca pudding, her favorite.

"Jesus!" I slammed pots and pans around, and Howard shivered with fear and happiness.

After dinner I called Reenie and told her yes. "Only for a couple of days," I said severely.

"Oh, you're a pal," she cried.

Later, she exclaimed over the pudding and threw Howard a knowing look. Was I a fool? But her bones pushed their knobs through her clothing. Her nostrils were red and crusty from a lingering cold. Under the table I found the sleek truth of my own thigh, and I grew calm again.

Of course the living room was closed to us for our nightly consultation. Reenie was there with a stack of magazines, a dish of that damn pudding, and the radio tuned to some distant and static-shot program.

I drew Howard into the bedroom and shut the door. It was my turn, and I settled into the year I was nine with a minimum of effort. It was a memorable year, because my parents were discussing a possible divorce on the other side of my bedroom wall. How was that for trauma? I was Gloria Vanderbilt, a subject of custody, an object of sympathy. I imagined myself little again, and I invented their conversation. *What about the kid?* my mother asked. *Oh, you're the one who always wanted a kid*, my father answered.

Next to me, Howard moved restlessly. "It's a good thing Reenie and I never had any children," he said.

"That's true," I conceded, and then I tried to continue my story, but Reenie coughed in the other room, two throat-clearing blasts that pinned us to the pillows.

"What's *that*?" Howard asked.

"Oh, for heaven's sake! You broke my train of thought again!"

"I only asked."

"Forget the whole thing. It's no use telling you anything anyway."

"Go ahead," he said, rubbing my back in conciliation. "Come on. Start from, 'Oh, you're the one who always wanted a kid.'"

"Forget it."

"Jesus!" he said. "Just feel this. My pulse is so slow, my blood must be like clay."

In the morning Reenie was watching the playground from the shelter of the curtains, like a gangster holed up in a hideout.

"I'm a wreck," she said. "I keep thinking that nut is going to come here."

"Why should he come here? How could he even know where you are?"

She didn't answer. She moved to the sink, where she squeezed fresh orange juice into a glass with her bare hands. I wished Howard could have seen that. The untapped strength of that girl!

Jason was a traitor. He ran kisses up her freckled arms. "My Weeny!" he cooed. They drank the unstrained juice in sips from the same glass.

Later, I went downstairs and called Howard at work from a pay phone. "She has to go."

"I know that. Don't you think I know that?"

"I mean forever."

"Well, what do you want *me* to do?"

"Nominate her for Miss Subways. Get her deported. I don't know. Why don't you find her a husband?"

"Ha-ha. Should I look in the Yellow Pages?"

"Well, *you* married her."

"That's another story," he said, but I refused to listen.

"Ask around," I said, and I hung up.

At home again, I tried my own hand. "Stand up straight. Give them both barrels." But the narrow points of her breasts thrust out like drill bits. "No, no, *relax*." I let her try on some of my clothes, but they enclosed her like tents. Instead, we worked on makeup and her psychological approach to men. But it all seemed useless. In ten minutes there were smudges under her eyes from the mascara and lipstick on her teeth.

"Relax," I told her. "That's the whole secret," and she collapsed in a slump as if her spinal cord had been severed.

That night Howard came home with a man from his office. I'd never seen him before. He wore dark glasses and he had a caustic smile: he was divorced, too, and spoke about getting burned once and never playing with fire again.

"Oh, *terrific,*" I whispered to Howard.

But he shrugged. He had done his share. Now it was up to me. I did the best I could, flaunting my marital joy at this stranger like a bullfighter's cape. But everything must have seemed bleak to him, through those dark glasses. My dinner was loaded with killer cholesterol, the apartment was overheated and confining, someone was deflating the tires on his car parked two blocks away.

Of course Reenie didn't help at all. She pretended to be our eldest child, and ate her French fries with her fingers. There was a huge pink stain on the front of her blouse.

"I'll call you," the man said to her when he left, a phrase torn from memory. We were all surprised that he bothered.

"You didn't have to," Reenie said to Howard later, as if he had brought her a frivolous but thoughtful gift.

In bed, Howard and I listened for night sounds from the other room, and we were rewarded. In her sleep Reenie called out, and I could feel Howard next to me, poised for flight on the edge of the mattress.

Dear Abby/Ann Landers/Dr. Rose Franzblau, What should I do? Signed, Miserable.

Dear Mis, Do you keep up with the national scene? Can you discuss things intelligently with your husband; i.e., name all the cabinet members, the National Book Award nominees, the discoverer of DNA? Have you looked in the mirror lately? Do you make the most of your natural good looks? Go to an art gallery, make an exciting salad for dinner, reline your kitchen shelves with wild floral paper. And good luck!

The days went by somehow and we began to settle in as if things were fine, as if Reenie *belonged* on our couch every night, leaving those shallow depressions in the cushions.

My mother called to offer some advice. "Get rid of her," she said.

My father picked up the bedroom extension and listened. I could hear the hiss of his breath.

"Hello, Dad," I said.

"Are you on, Herm?" my mother asked. "Is that you?"

My father cleared his throat right into the mouthpiece. He was going to offer advice as well, and his style was based on Judge Hardy in the old Mickey Rooney movies. Kindly. Dignified. Judiciously stern. All his days he sat for imaginary Bachrach portraits. In the subway, at the movies. "What I would do . . ." he said, and then he paused.

My mother waited. I waited. I tapped my foot on the kitchen tile.

"What should she do?" my mother insisted. "Should she throw her out the window? Should she stuff her in the incinerator?"

"I believe I was speaking," Judge Hardy said.

"Oh, pardon *me*," my mother said. "For living."

"What I would do," he began again, "is seek professional advice."

"Thanks, Dad."

"Yes," he said. "Professional advice." He paced in his chambers.

"It's not normal," my mother said. "It's not nice." Her opinion about other things as well—homosexuality, artificial insemination, and the hybridization of plants.

The next day I lent Reenie twenty dollars and looked through the classified ads for a new apartment for her. "Change your luck," I advised, like a fortune-teller.

When the children were napping, the doorbell rang. An eye loomed back at mine, magnified through the peephole. "Who?"

"Reenie there?"

My heart gave tentative leaps, like the first thrusts of life in a pregnancy. I opened the chains and bolts with shaky hands and ran inside. "It's a man," I hissed, rebuttoning Reenie's blouse, combing her hair with my fingers. But it was no use. She still looked neglected and ruined.

The man burst into the room.

"Oh, for God's sake, it's you!" Reenie said.

"I told you," he said. "When I want something, I go after it."

"Well, just piss off, Raymond."

"It's you and me, baby," he said. "All the way."

I watched from the doorway. He was a big ox of a man, the kind who invites you to punch him in the belly and then laughs at your broken hand. There was a cartoon character tattooed on his forearm—Yogi Bear or Smokey.

"Call the police," Reenie said wearily.

"The *police*?"

"Why fight nature, Reenie?" he asked.

"That's right," I said, winking at him.

"He's a lunatic," she explained. "He's the one I *told* you about. From Unemployment."

My hope began to ebb. "Well, you could just give him a *chance*."

Jason came in from the bedroom then, barefoot, squinting in the assault of new light. "Stop hollering," he said.

"My intentions are honorable," the lunatic said, crossing his heart. "Cute kid," he offered, about Jason.

I reached for that slender thread of hope. "Do you like children?" I asked.

He leaned on his wit. "Say, I used to be one myself!" He laughed and laughed, wiping tears from his eyes.

"Reenie, Reenie," I said. "Introduce me."

"He-has-a-prison-record," she sang in falsetto behind her hand.

They might have been political protest arrests, for all I knew, or something else that was fashionable. I snapped my fingers. "*Honi soit*," I said.

"Bad checks," Reenie said. She was relentless.

I always try to find the good in people and he had nice eyes, hazel with gorgeous yellow flecks. I offered him coffee and he accepted. Reenie sat down finally.

They were married two weeks later. Howard gave the bride away, which may not be traditional, but it meant a lot to me, for the symbolism. I gave them a silver-plated bread tray and sincere wishes for the future. Raymond had a lead on a job in Chicago and they left in a hailstorm of rice for the airport.

"That's that," I said, never believing it for a moment.

Two months later, Raymond showed up at the door at three o'clock in the morning. Things didn't work out, he said, by way of explanation. Reenie was staying in Chicago for a while, to seek new horizons, but she had promised to keep in touch.

Raymond's feet hung over the arm of the sofa when I tucked him in. He snored and the sofa springs groaned in rhythm with his dreams.

He looks through the want ads every day. He takes the garbage to the incinerator and he picks up the mail for us in the morning. My little talks with Howard are expanded into small but amiable group sessions now. Raymond's stories are interesting, as I might have suspected, from the tattoo and all. He never even knew his real parents or his true history. We sent him to NYU for a battery of aptitude tests and it seems that he might do well in social research or merchandising.

As for me, I have good days and bad. At the supermarket, I am dazzled by the bounty. In bed, I am a passenger, still ready for cosmic flight. My daily horoscope predicts smooth sailing ahead!

I worry about Reenie, though. Today there was an airmail letter. She is lonely and her body absorbs only the harmful additives in food. After all, Chicago is not her hometown.

(1974)

The Sex Maniac

Everybody said that there was a sex maniac loose in the complex and I thought—it's about time. It had been a long asexual winter. The steam heat seemed to dry all of the body's moistures and shrivel the fantasies of the mind. From the nineteenth floor of Building A, I watched snow fall on the deserted geometry of the playground. The colors of the world were lustless, forbidding. White fell on gray. Gray shadows drew over the white.

He was first seen in the laundry room of Building D, but it was not clear just how he had presented himself. Was his attack verbal, physical, visual? The police came and they wrote down in their notebooks the varying stories of the housewives. He was next seen near the incinerators on the sixth floor of our building. He was seen twice by elderly widows whose thin shrieks seemed to pierce the skull. There had been an invasion of those widows lately as if old men were dying off in job lots. The widows marched behind the moving men, fluttering, birdlike. Their sons and daughters were there to supervise, looking sleek and modern next to the belongings—chairs with curved legs, massive headboards of marriage beds trembling on the backs of the movers. The widows smiled shyly as if their survival embarrassed them.

Now two of them had encountered a sex maniac. Help, they had shrilled. Help and help and he had been frightened off by their cries. I wondered where he waited now in ambush and if I would meet him on a loveless February night.

There were plenty of men in my life that winter, not one of them a sex maniac. The children developed coughs that made them sound like seals barking, and the health plan sent a doctor. He was thin, mustachioed, and bowed with the grind of house calls. Bad boys in bad neighborhoods slashed his tires and snapped his aerial in two. Angry children bit his fingers as he pried open the hinges of their jaws. I clasped a flower pin to the bosom of my best housedress, the children jumped on the bed intoning nursery rhymes, but the doctor snapped his bag shut with the finality of the last word. His mustache narrow and mean, he looked just like the doctors of my childhood. We trailed after him to the door but he didn't turn around. Never mind. There were policemen to ask us leading questions. There was the usual parade of repairmen and plumbers.

There was the delivery boy from the market. His name is Earl. We coaxed him into the apartment. Just put it down there, Earl. Just wait a minute while I get my purse, Earl. Is it still as cold out there? we asked. Is it going to snow again? Do you think the price level index will rise? Will I meet the man of my dreams? Will I take a long voyage? But he was a boy without vision or imagination. He counted out the change and hurried to leave.

That night I said to Howard, "Love has left this land." When the children were tucked in behind veils of steam from the vaporizer, he tried to disprove it. He put his arms around me in that chorus of coughing and whispering radiators. But the atmosphere was more medicinal than romantic and the lovemaking was only ritual. It was no one's fault. It was the fault of the atmosphere, the barometric pressure, the wind velocity. We consoled each other in the winter night.

The next day the whole complex was thrumming with excitement. The sex maniac had been seen by a very reliable source. The superintendent's wife came from a mining area in Pennsylvania, a place not noted for frivolity. She had gazed at a constant landscape and she had known men who had suffocated in sealed mines. Her word was to be honored; she had no more imagination than the grocer's boy. After the police were finished, the women of the building fell on her with questions. Did he just—you know—show himself? Did he touch her? What did he say?

She answered with humorless patience. Contrary to rumor, he was a slight man, not very tall, and young, like her own son. But not really like her own son, she was quick to add. He had said terrible, filthy things to her in a funny, quiet way, as if he were praying, and I saw him in my mind's eye, reedy and pallid, saying his string of obscenities like a litany in a reverent and quaking voice.

I wondered who he was, after all, and why he had chosen us. Had he known instinctively that we needed him, that winter had chilled us in our hearts and our beds?

But the superintendent's wife said that he hadn't touched at all, only longed to touch, promised, threatened to touch.

Ahhh, cried the women. Ahhh. The old widows ran to the locksmith for new bolts and chains.

The men in the building began to do the laundry for their wives. They went in groups with their friends. Did the sound of their voices diminishing in the elevators remind the super's wife of men going down to the mines?

Did you see him? the wives asked later, and, flinging the laundry bags down, some of the husbands laughed and said, yes, he asked for you, he told me to give you this and this, and the wives shrieked with joy.

Howard ruined our clothes, mixing dark and white things, using too much bleach. But when he came back from the laundry room it was as if he had returned from a crusade.

"Have you heard anything?" I asked, and he smiled and said, "You don't need a sex maniac."

But you *were*, I thought. Your eyes and your hands used to be wild and your breath came in desperate gulps. You used to mumble your own tender obscenities against my skin and tell me that I drove you crazy. I looked at Howard, his hand poised now on the rim of the laundry basket, and I knew that I was being unfair. But whose love is not unfair? When is it ever reasonable?

Perhaps whatever I needed was outside the confines of the building, farther than the outer edges of the complex where I could see the grocer's boy on his bicycle turning in concentric circles toward our building. Artfully, he raised the front wheel as he rode on the rear one, and then the bicycle became level again like a prancing pony. "Whoa," I said against the windowpane, and then I waited for him to come up.

His ears were red from the cold wind. He snuffled and put the bag of groceries on the kitchen counter. He is the sort of boy who won't meet your eyes. His own, half-lidded and guarded, seemed to look at my feet. And because I didn't want him to go yet and didn't know what else to do, I said, "Have you heard about the sex maniac, Earl?"

The red of his ears flamed to his face and I thought he would be consumed by his own heat. He answered from the depths of his throat in a voice that might have been silent for weeks.

"Whaaa?" he asked.

There was no way to retreat. "The sex maniac," I said. "He stays in the complex. He molests women. *You* know."

Perhaps he did. But if he didn't, then a match had been set to his brain. His eyes opened wide, as if a startling idea had suddenly occurred to him. Sex maniac, he was thinking, and I watched his face change as the pictures rolled inside his head. Sex maniac! A grocery bag slid across the counter and into the bowl of the sink. But he stood there, his hand paused at the pocket of his vinyl jacket. Half-nude housewives lay in stairwells pleading for their release. Please don't, they begged. For God's sake, have mercy. His lips were moving, shaping melodies.

I pulled on the sleeve of his jacket. "Listen, did you bring the chow-chow?" I asked. "Look Earl, the oranges are all in the sink."

Slowly the light dimmed in his face. He looked at me with new recognition. "I always take good care of you, don't I?" he asked.

"Yes, you do," I assured him. "You're a very reliable person."

"What does this here guy do?"

"Who?"

"The whatchamacallit—the maniac."

I began to put the oranges back into the bag. "Oh gosh, I don't know. I never saw him. Who knows? Rumors build up. You know how they snowball."

"Yeah," he said, dreamy, distant.

"Well, so long," I said. I pressed the money into his relaxed hand.

"Yeah," he said again.

I guided him down the hallway and out through the door.

That evening the superintendent came to fix the leaking faucet in the bathtub. "Keeping to yourself?" he asked as he knelt on the bathroom tile.

I was surprised. He usually avoided conversation. "More or less," I said cautiously.

"You women better stick close to home," he advised.

"Oh, I *do*, I *do*," I said.

"You know what that guy said to the missus? You know the kind of language he used?" His eyes were a cruel and burning blue. He unscrewed a washer and let it fall with a clank into the tub. He raised his hand. "Do you know what I'll do if I catch that guy? Whop! Whop!" His hand became a honed razor, a machete, a cleaver. "Whop! Whop!"

I blinked, feeling slightly faint. I sat down on the edge of the closed toilet seat.

The superintendent replaced the washer and stood up. "You ever see him?" he asked.

I shook my head.

His long horny forefinger shot out and pushed against my left nipple as if he were ringing a doorbell. "Maybe he don't go for a big woman," he said, and lumbered through the doorway.

I sat there for a few minutes and then I went into the kitchen to start supper.

Several days went by and gradually people stopped talking about the sex maniac. He seemed to have abandoned the complex. It was as if he hadn't been potent enough to penetrate the icy crusts of our hearts. Poor harmless thing, I thought, but at least he had tried.

The children's coughs abated and I took them to the doctor's office for a final checkup. He examined them and scribbled something on their health records. "Did they ever catch that fellow?" he asked suddenly.

"I don't think so," I said.

"Did he actually attempt *assault*?" the doctor asked. I must have seemed surprised because he poked at his mustache and said, "I've always had an interest in crimes of a sexual nature."

I dropped my eyes.

"I'm concerned with the psychodynamic origin of that kind of obsession." he persisted.

Aha, I said to myself. I stood up, smoothing the skirt of my dress. His eyes followed my gesture, lingering, and I thought, so here's my chance if I want one. Here's unlicensed desire. Was this where the sex maniac had led me?

"Oedipal complex, all that jazz," said the doctor, but his gaze stayed on my hips and his hands became restless on the desk.

But this wasn't what I had meant at all, not those clinical hands that tapped, tapped their nervous message. I could see the cool competence in his eyes, the first-class mechanic at home in his element, but it wasn't what I needed. He had nothing to do with old longings and the adolescent rise and plunge of the heart. He had no remedies for the madness of dreams or the sanity of what was familiar and dear.

"I once considered a residency in psychiatry," he said and he laughed nervously and glanced up at his wall of diplomas as if for reassurance.

Nothing doing, I thought, not a chance. But I laughed back just to show no hard feelings. I walked to the door and the doctor followed. "So long," I told him in a voice as firm and friendly as a handshake.

"Keep an eye on those tonsils," he said, just to change the subject.

The children and I went out into the meager sunlight. Filthy patches of snow melted into the pavement.

Home, I thought, home, as if it were my life's goal to get there. We walked toward the bus stop. Everywhere color was beginning to bleed through the grayness and I felt a little sadness. I had never seen him. Not once crouched in the corner of the laundry room, not once moaning his demands on the basement ramp, not once cutting footprints across the fresh snow in the courtyard. It was as if he had never existed. The winter was almost over and I was willing to wait for summer to come again.

Pulling the children along, although there was no one waiting for me, I began to run.

(1970)

Trophies

Howard's father died, moving Howard up one generation and canceling forever his coming attractions of life.

His father had been a gloomy man given to terrible bulletins of what it was like to be forty or fifty or sixty. Howard has untimely gray hairs and he's worried about growing old. Promises of pensions, matured insurance policies, and senior citizens' discounts don't cheer him at all.

"Distinguished one minute, extinguished the next," Howard says.

I can't argue with that.

Sometimes he does exercises in the morning. Slowly, slowly, like Lazarus, he rises into sit-ups, pulling his prospects into shape. He nibbles sunflower seeds, sowing them into furrows under the sofa cushions, and he cannot in good conscience eat eggs anymore. Instead, he eats honey and wheat germ and remarks on the early deaths of famous nutritionists. They die the same ways we do, Howard says, even in car wrecks and floods.

Now his father was dead of natural causes.

I helped Howard pack a suitcase so that he could visit his mother in Florida for a few days and prepare her for survival. "Why doesn't your sister go instead of you?" I asked.

"You know Marsha and her back. And she's never been good with death."

"Look who's talking," I said, but he didn't seem to hear me.

"Why are you packing *these*?" he demanded, pulling out his bathing trunks and the T-shirt with crossed tennis rackets on the pocket.

"It's hot down there," I said. "You're going to *Florida*."

"I'm not going for fun, you know." He crammed other things into the suitcase instead: scratchy wool sweaters, dark socks for the sober business of mourning—forcing New York and winter, the gloom of subways and museums, in with his underwear.

"We'll keep in touch," he promised, and the children and I stayed in the airline terminal until the plane lifted him away.

Back in the apartment again, things weren't so bad. I made a baked eggplant for supper, something I like that Howard hates. I slept in the middle of the bed, using both pillows. I kept all the lights on, a childhood luxury.

Still, Howard was everywhere: his fingerprints in wild profusion on the furniture, his Gouda cheese gathering mold in the refrigerator, the memory of his sleeping hand on my hip. All night I was a sentry waiting for morning. The children slept hopefully on the other side of the wall.

In the daytime I sat with the other mothers in the playground. The baby slept under cold sweet blankets in her carriage, and I rocked her with an aimless rhythm, like a tic. Jason was in the sandbox, among friends. They poured sand into his cupped hands, and it slid down the front of his nylon snowsuit. All around me my potential friends sat on benches. On the bench facing me there were three women in bright winter coats and scarves. Every once in a while their chattering voices and ripples of laughter came to me on currents of air, like birdsong. I thought I could fall asleep listening to them, feeling as peaceful and drugged as I do when Howard combs my hair.

I looked up and found our kitchen window nineteen stories up. I marked it with an X the way vacationers mark their hotel rooms on postcards.

Having a wonderful time. Wish you were here.

In the laundry room the man from apartment 16J was waiting for his wash to be finished. There was something intimate in our sitting together like that, watching his sheets tangled and thrashing like lovers in the machine. Pajamas, nightgowns, towels mingling, drowning.

We smiled at each other but we didn't speak. His wife, I'd heard, was a cold, unsmiling woman. But he looked like a passionate man. You can tell sometimes by the urgency of gestures and by the eyes. His wife works at the DMV and he's home alone all day because of some on-the-job compensation case. He jammed his laundry, still damp and unfolded, into a pillowcase and he left.

What part of him was wounded or damaged?

That night Howard called from Florida. We shouted to each other over the distance of rooftops and highways.

"How is your mother?" I asked.

"It's very sad down here," he said.

His mother pulled the phone from his hand.

"Your husband is your best friend in the world!" she shouted.

Then Howard was back on the line. "They had two of everything. Place mats. Heating pads. BarcaLoungers."

"You were his favorite!" his mother cried to me, currying false indulgence for the dead.

Of course it wasn't true. If such things can be measured, I may well have been Howard's father's least favorite. He tried to buy me off right before the wedding with two hundred dollars and a bonus trip to the Virgin Islands. Irony wasn't his strong suit. Did he think my chastity might be restored there?

Bygones.

"What can I say?" I said.

Then Howard spoke. "I'm trying to straighten things out. It could take a few extra days. It's really sad here." He kept his voice low, but it sounded sun-nourished, tropical.

Later the phone rang again and this time it was a breather. I figured it had to be that love-locked man in 16J. The woman he was married to would never submit to ecstasy. Instead, she was the prison matron of his lust, the keys to everything hanging just out of reach below her waist.

Did 16J know Howard was away? News travels fast in these big buildings.

"Who is this?" I demanded, but he chose to remain silent, to contain his longings for other days, better times.

One day the children and I went to visit my mother and father. Everything in their apartment was covered in plastic: lampshades, sofas, chairs. Photographs tucked away in mirror frames and on tables. The specter of death was there and I embraced my father in a wrestler's hold.

"How are you!" I cried.

"Don't worry about him," my mother said. "He's not going anyplace."

"I'm in the pink," my father admitted.

Back home again, Howard called and I tried to keep things light. "We all miss you," I said. "We've had colds. Jason wanted to know if your plane crashed."

"The kid said that?" Howard asked. He spoke soothing words to Jason. I held the receiver to the baby's ear, too.

"It snowed again," I told Howard.

He said it was murderously hot in Florida and there were jellyfish in the water. He had to wear his father's swim trunks.

"This business could break your heart," he said.

16J's wife came to collect money to combat a terrible disease.

"Come right in," I said. "Why don't you sit down."

I went to get my purse, leaving her stone-faced, alone with the children. Did she suspect anything? Had she come to give fair warning? What would she say, this gauleiter of pleasure?

But she said nothing. After she left the apartment, I looked for messages, for words printed in furniture dust.

But there was only my receipt for the donation and a pamphlet telling why I should have given more.

It's lonely here, I thought. Quiet as an aftermath. Howard's presence was fading. Only the Gouda cheese, unspeakable now. I remembered that his mother had never liked me, either. She used to send Howard to the store for Kotex to remind him of her powers. She bought him a meerschaum pipe and a spaniel puppy to divert his course. But I was triumphant anyway.

Now I imagined a thousand and one Floridian nights, the air conditioner humming in orchestral collusion with her voice, her voice buying time. She had an armory of ammunition, steamer trunks stuffed with Howard's child-hood. In my head I canceled the air conditioner; she fanned him with a palm leaf instead, a cool maternal zephyr on his burnished head.

"So, where was I?" she asks.

Howard's hair lifts lightly in the breeze. His eyes shut. Her voice shuffles into his sleep, into mine.

In the middle of the night I heard footsteps in the hallway outside the apartment. Then, an eloquent silence. I tiptoed to the door, pressed my ear against it.

"Who's there?" I whispered. "Is it you?"

But no one answered. Deferred passion could drive a man crazy. He would probably want klieg lights to match the intensity of his craving, and a million weird variations on the usual stuff. His sheets in the washing machine were green, I remembered. Small scattered flowers on a limitless green field.

I went back to bed and let my blood settle. Maybe it was my motherhood he coveted. There are men like that, childless themselves, who long for the affirmation of new life around them. Between a woman's thighs they can either be coming or going, just delivered into the world or willing to leave it in one exquisite leap of desire.

Spring threatened, and my mother said, "He's taking his sweet time about coming home."

"Things are bad there," I said. "You know Florida."

"I know one thing," she said darkly.

I called Howard, but no one answered. I let the phone ring fifty times. They were walking together under palm trees, their faces dappled with sunlight and shadow. Later, they would go marketing, just enough for the two of them. Then they would rest on the BarcaLoungers.

The man in 16J paced restlessly in his apartment, a convertible studio with a gloomy exposure. The incinerator door clanged. Children's voices rose from the playground.

I played a hundred games of solitaire, but I never won. Later, I found the ten of hearts under the mattress in the baby's crib.

The next day I called Howard again. His mother answered the phone. They were just going to have lunch. I could hear dishes clatter, water running.

"What's up?" Howard asked. He wondered why I was calling before the rates changed.

"There's this man," I said.

"Who? What? I can't hear you, wait a minute." The background noises subsided.

"A madman!" I screamed at a splintering pitch. Then softly, "I'm afraid he's fallen in love."

"What!" Howard shouted. "Has he touched you? My God, did you let him?"

"It hasn't come to that," I said. "Not yet."

The plane circled for two hours before it came down. Howard looked like a movie star, tanned and radiant. The children wriggled to get to him. He carried a cardboard box under his arm. Souvenirs, I thought. Presents. A miniature crate of marzipan oranges. A baby alligator for Jason.

When we were in the car, Howard opened the box. There were no presents. There were just some things of his father's that his mother wanted him to have. Shoe trees. A weathered golf cap. An old street map of Chinatown and the Bowery. It was a grab bag of history, her final weapon.

Oh, it had seemed so easy. The car was stuck in an endless ribbon of traffic. My hand rested on Howard's knee, and the children were asleep in the back seat. I would have settled for just this, all of us stopped in time.

But Howard sighed. "A man has to live," he said.

(1975)

Bodies

Michael and Sharon Fortune are too young to have ever seen Lenny Bruce in performance, but they have vintage editions of Bruce's records, on which he denies vulgarity in anything sexual. There are no dirty words. And there are no dirty acts, except for the insidious ones of social injustice.

At the end of one record there's something about a flasher, a man who opens his raincoat and displays a bunch of lilacs instead of a penis. Like the trick of a gentle magician, Sharon thought the first time she heard it, and the visual image has stayed with her. Because she is an artist, all words convert finally into pictures; even her dreams are a silent, colorful banner of visual events.

Michael interviews elderly welfare applicants, and Sharon believes he is a vessel for language, a Steinberg cartoon figure composed of the hard-luck stories of strangers and his own urgent, unspoken words.

He's only the second lover she's ever had. The first was a prose poet named Beau Carpenter, and she met Michael on the rebound from that affair. The difference between the two men astounded her. Beau had been so authoritative, and she such a willing follower. She would wait in the wings of their bed for her cue to enter, apprentice to a master in a complicated acrobatic act. Not that Michael was passive. But he always made room for a fair, healthy share of her aggression, and sometimes Sharon was surprised to find herself raucously sexual.

With Beau, she had affected silence because he required it. After two years of marriage to Michael, she still questions him as if *she* were the social worker, and he had come to her for aid. He'd had the worst childhood she could imagine. And he spoke about it, when asked, with an almost detached calm. The family had lived in the Midwest. His mother was the breadwinner, a practical nurse who traveled around, staying in other people's houses to care for newborn infants. His father, once a Linotype operator, was housebound with severe emphysema. The rooms were clogged with his breathing. Michael was their only child, an easy target for his father's maniacal revenge on the world.

When Michael was about four or five years old, he told her, his father held his small hands over the open gas jets on the stove until his palms were scorched, until they cooked and blistered, a lesson on the dangers of playing with matches.

Sharon had cried out in an agony of compassion. "I'd like to *kill* him!"

"Too late," Michael said. "He's already dead."

"Well, what did your mother do about it?"

"She wasn't there. I guess she was out on a case."

"But she must have seen your hands when she came home."

Michael shrugged. "I don't remember," he said. "Maybe they were healed by then, I don't know. She came back every few weeks, dying for sleep, and headed for bed."

"Terrible," Sharon said, and he thought she meant for his mother.

"Yeah. She used to wake up and she couldn't remember where she was. She'd forget sometimes if a baby was a boy or a girl until she diapered it again."

"You must have hated your father."

"Yes."

Sharon stared at him. "Michael, why are you smiling?" she asked.

His mother died suddenly, of a stroke, and Michael flew to Dayton to take care of the funeral. While he was there, he rented a car and then decided to drive it all the way home. When the phone rang that night, she thought it was Michael, sleepless and lonely, calling from a motel room. But it was their lawyer friend Dick Schaffner.

She was working, finishing the last in a series of political cartoons. She clamped the receiver between her chin and her shoulder and continued to ink the drawing in front of her. Then she said, "What? *What?*" as if the connection had been broken or her hearing had failed, so that Dick was forced to shout the details at her. As she listened, she scribbled nervous markings all over her drawing, ruining it.

Dick told her to try to keep things in perspective, that it was pretty complicated, in a legal sense. "And it's not even supposed to be really sexual, you know," he said.

Of *course* she knew, and felt both tenderness and irritation at his affectionate condescension.

But despite everything, she clung to the idea that it *was* sexual, part of the whole damn business of bodies to which all psychic suffering can probably be traced. What else is it if a man takes his prick out in a public place and invites a strange woman to look at it?

She was alternately cold with shock and blazing with humiliation. She had been this way once before, when Beau left her for that other woman. The analogy was all wrong, but she felt stubbornly logical. *This* was a kind of jilting, too. She had become as ludicrous as those poor women who wrote desperate letters to advice columnists. It seemed to her that men never wrote to them for counsel in the love department, anymore than they asked anyone for directions.

★   ★   ★

Now Sharon is flying to Ohio because she urgently wants to go, and because Dick said that the presence of an attractive, supportive wife is invaluable in cases like this. He added, half-seriously, that if she were pregnant or could muster up a kid or two for the trip, it would even be better. Would she like to rent one of his? His office was going to make travel arrangements for her, and he would follow on a later flight and meet her there.

Sharon wishes that Dick was beside her now, holding her hand in one of his bear's paws and shuffling through official papers with the other. Instead, she has the aisle seat next to a man with tortuously styled hair, who is drinking a Scotch sour and staring out the window as if he were communing with Saint-Exupéry. Sharon has refused a drink; in a couple of hours she will be in a motel room where she can smoke one of the joints she has hidden in a cigarette pack, and be soothed.

Across the aisle an elderly woman, dressed resolutely in black—dress, scarf, stockings, shoes—is asleep. Italian, probably, or maybe Greek. She looks like a billboard for death. Why is it always the women in those places who are assigned the work of perpetual mourning?

After Beau left her, Sharon had plunged into mourning, too. Not inaccurately, or even unkindly, he predicted a full, formal year of grieving for her. She'd wondered if this was based on his own past experience or whether it was an absolute standard for female behavior in that kind of situation. That's how naïve she was in those days. But obediently she began to grieve, to start to get it over with. In a few weeks, she was able to think about him again. It wasn't that grief had become less, but that it had become different, moving up into the intellect, away from the body, from those aching places, the shoulders and the fingertips.

She is trying to focus on Michael, and it's his body she thinks of first, or bodies in general, a commuter's crowd of them in which his appears looking reasonable, if mortal. Cautiously, she imagines him clothed: the singing corduroy of his trousers as he walks, that yellow shirt. Sharon remembers the work of the cartoonist after whom she'd first fashioned herself stylistically, and who undressed everyone in the mind's eye of his characters. She does that sometimes, too, in life. Not for the sake of humor, though, or even for democracy; there is no democracy anyway. Sharon is tall and the woman Beau went off with is petite, and so on.

But she is unable to undress Michael now, must keep him protectively, lawfully covered. Instead she considers what has happened, what might happen next. The night before, after she had recovered a little, she called Dick back. Her voice was tremulous and uncertain, but her questions were not. "Why didn't he call me, too? Did he say, did he actually *say* that he did it?"

Dick sighed deeply and Sharon realized that it was very late and that he was probably in bed beside Anna. "We didn't go into it, Sharon," he said. "It's never a good idea, on the telephone. And he was allowed only one brief call, like in the movies. You know how that goes; they always call their mouthpiece."

"But why can't he be released until the arraignment? Isn't that what usually happens?" She hesitated and her voice fell into a hoarse whisper. "He doesn't have a record or anything, does he?"

"No, babe, no. Of course not. It's just that his timing was lousy for this particular place. There's been a series of assorted complaints over the past month or so. So they've invented a few extra charges to hold him on."

"That's not fair!" she cried.

"Fair!" Dick said. "Are you kidding? What does fair have to do with anything? Don't worry, Sharon. Come on. We'll get them to drop them all. We'll get the best local counsel. Everything will be okay."

"Did he explain that he was only driving through? Did he tell them about his mother?"

"Yeah, he explained everything. But the locals are still uneasy. And suspicious. They've *all* just buried their mother, and they don't know our Mikey the way we do."

But now Sharon didn't know him, either. "What kind of complaints?" she asked.

"What?"

"You said before—assorted complaints."

"Oh. An attempted rape in the Laundromat. Kids talking about a guy who hangs around the schoolyard."

"Oh, God, it wasn't a child, was it?" Sharon has always been sternly moralistic about what adults do to children. She might even have to cast the first stone herself. She remembered a drawing she did for a newspaper decrying inadequate security in city schools, after a child had been molested in a stairwell. Her version of the molester lurked in shadows, a grotesque, subhuman figure.

But Dick reassured her. "No, no. I *told* you. A grown woman." He said it in the condoning way one says "consenting adults," and he added, "In the parking lot of a supermarket."

"She could be lying, couldn't she? Or hallucinating?"

"Sure," Dick said, but his tone was palliative, and the details finally stunned her into silence.

"Are you okay?" Dick asked. "Listen, do you want me to bring Anna over to spend the rest of the night?"

And then Anna took the phone and asked a few gentle questions in a sleepy voice.

"No, I'm fine," Sharon said. "Really." And she did feel better, not only because there wasn't a child involved, but because the situation was becoming less real again. Men, *other* men, did that sort of thing in subway passages, or in dark alleyways. The parking lot of a supermarket seemed foolishly domestic for such an unnatural gesture.

Yet suddenly she pictured Michael unfolding to his height from the car. He was stopping for cigarettes, probably, on the way to a motel. And she pictured the woman, also, midthirties, darkly pretty, wheeling one of those recalcitrant shopping carts, or juggling too many grocery bags and trying to find the car keys, and thinking of dinner and what to do about her elderly widowed father, and recalling a fleeting lust for her minister, and then seeing Michael.

Public nudity still surprises Sharon. When she was sixteen, she took a life drawing class. She was late for the first session and arrived after the model was arranged in her pose on the platform. How flagrant her nakedness seemed; she loomed so large Sharon could not fit her onto the newsprint page. Sometimes her feet were missing, sometimes her head. After several poses, the model put on a robe and wandered among the easels smoking a cigarette. Sharon felt embarrassed and apologetic, as if she were witnessing the aftermath of the primal scene. And she knew again the frustration of not knowing anything, with the underlying fear that it was not due to her youth, but to some fatal flaw that would keep her from the world's mysteries forever. She smoked one of the model's cigarettes and said pretentious things about form and space. Later the bare breasts stared at her with contempt.

The plane dips slightly and Sharon presses back against a wave of vertigo. The man in the window seat looks at her inquiringly, and she shakes her head and shuts her eyes.

Oh, consider passion for a moment! Dick has assured her that Michael's is not a crime of passion. And once she couldn't wait to agree with Beau that it all begins in the head and then sends its orders rushing down through the nerves and into the bloodstream, arousing the troops, those mercenaries. But when he told her that the first thing he admired about her was her eyesight, she was bewildered, wanting only to be wanted in more conventional ways. Why not admire her blondeness, which was everywhere, or her buttocks, which were worthy of praise?

But soon she learned to feel cherished and, covering each eye in turn, read aloud to him the small print of a sign on the other side of the Williamsburg Bridge. Acting further in kind, she told him that his feet pleased her. Vision and stride. An uncommon attraction, but stirringly original.

All right, she decides, forget passion. It's really comfort she's trying to think of in bodily terms, anyway. How each of us starts out bravely alone, lover and beloved at once, and works toward the ultimate collaboration, that other serious presence in the darkness. Is it that she always fails in this connection, or that Michael is hopelessly wounded, inconsolable?

When the flight attendant comes down the aisle offering newspapers, Sharon takes one. But she cannot concentrate on the headlines, on the larger, shared tragedies of fires, famine, and politics. She reads a small article on an inside page. It says that scientists have discovered that the bones of fat people are especially dense and sturdy. As she reads it, she thinks of Michael and his thinness. She imagines his bones (a murderous urge and a longing), and they are as delicate and as porous as coral, yet unable to resist the loping curve of his posture. His breastbone is an archer's bow.

Early that morning, Sharon had awakened abruptly and in a panic. "I can't, I *can't*," she said, not sure what she meant, but feeling more desperate for distraction than for interpretation. Thought was treacherous. Getting out of bed might require major effort. To delay it she took a magazine from the nightstand and opened it at random to an interview with Sartre, by Simone de Beauvoir. He said, "We yield our bodies to everyone, even beyond the realm of sexual relations: by looking, by touching."

Tell that to the judge, she thinks now, wishing she could be convinced of it herself. Maybe she will be when she is in her seventies, like Sartre.

Her seatmate gets up to go to the bathroom. His legs brush over Sharon's and he murmurs, "Excuse me," but he winks.

When he returns, she rises to let him pass.

"Business or pleasure?" he asks, and she looks at him blankly.

"In Columbus," he says.

"I'm meeting my husband there. Not really there, farther east, on the outskirts. His mother just died," she adds, and is horrified to realize she is smiling.

He smiles back. "What does your husband do?"

Do? He's in zippers. He pops flies. He shows his choice goods to discriminating shoppers.

"He's a social worker," she says, "with the city's welfare system."

The man continues to smile, not registering her answer. He's had a second drink, and maybe still another in the john from a flask, and she can see that he has a buzz on. He leans back in his seat and faces her intimately, as if they are sharing a bed pillow. He is wearing the kind of suit she most dislikes, with very large lapels and contrasting piping, and he has exaggerated sideburns. He looks like a member of a barbershop quartet, or like Captain Kangaroo. Yet she understands that he imagines himself attractive to her, sexy.

She goes through the mind process that removes his offending clothing, a piece at a time. Off with the jacket, with the busy tie. Off with the shiny synthetic shirt that clutches his bull neck in a stranglehold. She drops his trousers and they fall to his ankles, clanking keys and loose change everywhere. Impatiently, she pulls off his stacked-heel shoes, his socks, his plaid boxers, even the chains that protect his slack and hairy chest from evil with amulets from three separate cultures. But when he sits there at last, heavy-eyed with seduction and whiskey, the seat belt strapped across his puckered navel, just above his nodding cock, his body is as absurd to her as his clothing. Quickly, she dresses him again and turns away.

Michael always undressed without shyness or seduction, a practical business before bath or bed, as if he were unconscious of how well he was made, or of his easy athletic grace. And Sharon resisted what she considers a crude tendency toward voyeurism. He isn't the first man she's ever seen, though, and maybe he won't be the last.

Once it was her goal in life. Father and grandfather dead before memory, she lived in a household of females: grandmother, aunt, mother, older sister. They undressed openly, too, offering Sharon the various stages of her future, and she was interested, but of course she wasn't satisfied. Word was out.

She had seen statues of men at the Brooklyn Museum, budding in marble, bloodless and chaste. Their eyes were absent, too. At the circumcision of a neighbor's infant when Sharon was four, someone turned her face to the wall at the last minute. "Don't look," the woman said, a good beginning for a fairy tale with moral significance if Sharon had not been consistently obedient, had not shielded those 20/20 eyes and counted until it was over. But just before the ritual, she watched closely and saw that the baby's parts were still wrinkled from passage, and she heard him cry piteously, as if he were intolerably afflicted.

And she had a male dog for a while during childhood. He was a small mixed breed with a coarse brown coat and an affectionate nature. She called him Prince. She would take him into bed in the morning and stroke his belly and ears, and he would loll, sighing. Once, while she petted him, a thin red tube emerged from that hair-tipped pinch of flesh with the startling clarity of her sister's first lipstick. Sharon picked him up quickly and roughly and put him on the floor. "Bad dog!" she scolded, uncoached, and Prince growled at her.

The first naked man she ever saw was a friend's father, after Sharon slept at their house one night in the summertime. He must have been about thirty-five or forty years old. Sharon opened the door to her friend's parents' bedroom in the morning, mistaking it for the door to the bathroom. There was that particularly early stillness, the clockwork pause before life resumes. The mother was asleep, and the father was just getting up. He stood, in profile to Sharon, stretching his arms overhead, and then sat down on the edge of the bed, holding a pair of shorts in one hand. He seemed to be daydreaming.

He was a depressed man. Years later he committed suicide. In those days, though, he was only eccentric and moody, given to sardonic remarks that were hurtful to others. Sharon was afraid of him in an instinctive way; he had never been cruel to her, had hardly noticed her.

But in that quick and brilliant moment—she is sure she remembers sunlight in the bedroom—she saw his melancholy in the droop of his genitals, and felt a rush of knowledge and of anguish.

★ ★ ★

She hurries from the plane as if she is going to be met by friends or loved ones. Other passengers are greeted and she moves past their pleasured cries and embraces to an exit from the terminal and a taxi.

She gives the driver the name of the motel and sits back.

"Well, hello, *hello!*" he says, and bending one sunburned and tattooed arm onto the ledge of his open window, he pulls away from the curb with the tires screeching.

In the past, Sharon had been mildly annoyed by this kind of silly attention from men, the construction-worker syndrome of whistles, catcalls, and general showing off. It was a kind of harmless, universal foreplay. But now it seems like such Stone Age behavior, one step beyond chest-thumping. She feels much worse than annoyed—imposed upon. Who asked for this?

The cab driver sings, leans on the horn needlessly, and watches Sharon in the rearview mirror so that he has to brake sharply for a squirrel that decides to cross the road. "Fucker," he mutters, and goes forward again, but more slowly this time, his spirit tamed.

The motel is the same one Michael had gone to, after, and where he was arrested. Dick had made reservations for himself and her there, but it is not a thoughtless choice. The rented Ford is still parked there, and the place is clean and convenient to the jail where Michael is being held. Early tomorrow, she and Dick will go there together for the only visitation permitted before arraignment.

The motel manager's face gives nothing away when she claims her reservation. Behind him, a door opens briefly and she can see a living room and two small children watching television before it closes again. She signs the registration slip and has an urge to ask to see the one Michael must have signed the day before. How does a man feel after such an act? Frightened? Exhilarated? So deeply affected perhaps that his handwriting is irrevocably altered. And there is the keener fantasy that it will be another man's signature altogether, one of those wonderful minor news stories about mistaken identity. Families of men killed in the war and sent home in sealed coffins must suffer that possibility over and over again.

But she asks for nothing but the key to her room and the one to the car.

The room is shabbily genteel and telescopically smaller than the one depicted on the postcards for sale in the motel office. There are twin beds with green covers, and matching drapes that transform the last of an Ohio sunset into a Martian luminescence.

Dick's flight won't be in until seven thirty, and he has instructed her to stay put, not to drive to the airport to meet him; he will come directly to the motel and they can go out for dinner and talk about the next day.

There are almost two hours ahead during which she will be alone in this place and she contemplates them with increasing nervousness. She rejects the idea of smoking pot, losing confidence in its shamanistic powers to thwart loneliness. She knows intuitively that this is a dangerous time of day when, for some people, blood sugar plummets, and fatigue is a marauder. If records were to be checked, she is sure there would be a disproportionate number of suicides, automobile accidents, and violent crimes committed just before dusk. Brooders begin to gather evidence for their brooding. Insomniacs think of scary darkness, depressives of death.

Sharon opens the drapes and her room faces a small swimming pool surrounded by a locked cyclone fence. A few children run crazily around it, shrieking and hurling scraps of paper at one another that blow back into their own faces. She wonders what Michael is doing at this moment and thinks how awkward it will be to see him in that place, with this new knowledge between them. She feels that changes are taking place inside her, as mysterious and involuntary as metabolism and circulation. What if she experiences a complete failure of love, even of charity? She closes the drapes, making the room green again, and lies down on the bed nearest the window. Now she regrets not having brought along something to read, even the complimentary magazine from the seat pocket in the plane.

On the night table next to her, a pictorial breakfast menu from the motel's coffee shop is propped against an ashtray. Glorified color photos of eggs and sausage, of waffles and pancakes, looking more like Oldenburg sculptures of food than like real food, are advertised at irregular prices, as if they had been marked down: $1.79 for The Sunrise Special, $2.05 for Old Macdonald's Choice. She reads a printed message from the maid thanking her for being such a wonderful guest, and it is hand signed in a childishly broad scrawl: *Sincerely, Wanda.*

Sharon looks at her watch and then holds it to her ear to confirm its function. With her splendid vision she can read the sign on the back of the door at least eight feet from the bed. Checkout time, she learns, is at 11:00 A.M., and there is a map showing the locations of the laundry room and the ice machine.

In the drawer of the night table Sharon finds a thin phone book for the local area, and the mandatory Bible. She opens the phone book to see if there is anyone listed with the same name as Michael or herself. If there is, she decides, she will take that as a good omen for tomorrow. There isn't, but she finds a Richard Schaffner and someone with a spelling variation of her father's name living on Sharon Court. *That* could mean something, couldn't it? She wonders about the woman who saw Michael in the parking lot the day before, and if she is listed in the telephone book, too. Sharon imagines calling the number just to hear her voice, and then hanging up again without speaking.

Michael had called her a few hours after his mother's funeral. He sounded fine at first and then his voice became softer and fainter as if he were traveling swiftly away on a boat or a train, and twice she had to ask him to speak louder. He said that a few neighbors had come to the chapel, and the woman his mother lived with, another practical nurse, had gone to the cemetery with him. She wore her uniform and those rubber-soled shoes. She said that his mother had died from the babies, from sleeping in those small rooms they gave you, and the babies used up all the air. She complained bitterly about eating tainted luncheon meat while the family ate steak, about having only a tiny corner of a closet in which to hang her uniforms, next to stored luggage, ironing boards, and folded bridge tables.

She was crazy. She said she dreamed of poisoning babies or drowning them and what was she supposed to do now that his mother wouldn't be sharing the rent on their apartment; she couldn't afford it. And young couples didn't even wait six weeks postpartum anymore she could hear them going at it through the walls at night.

When he left, she followed right behind him, her shoes squeaking. He gave her some money for a taxi that she tucked into her pocket without even looking at it, and she kept walking alongside the car and talking to him as he drove slowly away. He was afraid she would fall under the wheels.

"I should have come with you," Sharon said. "You should have let me."

"No," he insisted. "It's all right. I handled it. You had a deadline anyway—"

"But I wanted to," she said, which wasn't really true. Maybe she still resented his mother for not protecting him from his father.

"Well, it's fine, it's all settled now. I'm on my way," he told her. "I'll be home soon."

The telephone book slides to the floor and Sharon opens the Bible to Ecclesiastes and reads. "Sorrow is better than laughter, for by the sadness of the countenance the heart is made better."

When Beau was packing his books, she watched him silently for a while, still reflexively aiming to please. Then she said, in her new, diminished voice, "And what did you admire about *her*, first?"

One of his hands rested on a volume of John Donne; with the other he took off his glasses and rubbed his eyes. "The usual," he said. "Her breasts, her skin."

She closes the Bible and puts it back into the night table drawer. Her hand goes to her heart, to her breast, and then up to the dependable pulse of her throat.

Last year, when her aunt had her breast removed, Sharon went to the hospital to visit her. And they did not talk about the breast, as if it were a mutual friend who had done something offensive and was suddenly in disfavor. They talked about Sharon and Michael instead, and her aunt confessed shyly that she had never liked the other fellow, that poet Sharon used to go out with, and that she was relieved when Sharon and Michael were safely married. And Sharon had begun to brag, exaggerating Michael's virtues. She told her aunt that it was she who had broken up with Beau and that he had begged and pleaded for another chance. She took extraordinary pleasure in her aunt's approval, in the lying itself, and in her own intact flesh later that night.

There is a knocking at the door and she realizes she has been asleep. It is past eight o'clock. Dick comes into the room and hugs her. His large mustache scrapes her face and his embrace is amazingly solid.

They drive to a restaurant in the rented car, and Sharon's appetite is much better than she expected. In fact, she eats everything on her plate and some of Dick's dinner, too. He's confident things will work out well the next day. They share a full bottle of Chablis, and there is an inappropriate air of celebration. Dick has done some research. He's been reading up on the subject and has even called a couple of shrinks he knows. A single, isolated episode of exhibitionism, he tells her, especially following a trauma like the death of one's mother, doesn't have to be pathological in origin. He was standing next to his car. There is reasonable consideration about his wish to be apprehended through license plate identification. And did she know that indecent exposure occurs most frequently in the spring?

"A young man's fancy?" she says, and is further loosened by Dick's laughter. Oh oh, she thinks.

Back at the motel, she asks him to come to her room to continue talking.

He looks at her speculatively and then follows her inside. "Only for a few minutes," he says. "I want to be sparkling in the morning. So you won't be sorry you didn't bring F. Lee Bailey instead."

She takes the pack of cigarettes from her purse and empties it carefully onto one of the beds. She selects the joints and shows them to Dick.

"Oy," he says, clapping his forehead. "Do you want to get us busted, too?" Then he takes matches from his pocket and lights one.

It's potent stuff, as promised, or perhaps the wine has eased the way. They become high quickly. Sharon feels uncommonly happy and hopeful. But even as she considers this blissful new state, she senses a sobering one approaching from a great distance, like a storm.

What if I come down too quickly? she thinks. What if Dick's optimism is artificially induced, too? She tries to remember if he was this cheerful and reassuring before dinner. What if he wants to make love to me? And she knows that it is her own desire she contemplates.

Dick takes off his jacket and falls into a chair, lifting his feet onto the bed. He is barrel-chested, growing a little portly.

Sharon is touched by what she sees as the body's first small concession to aging. She takes off her shoes and lies down on the bed, her feet almost touching Dick's.

"Freud gave up sex at forty," Dick says. "My friend Marshall says he was probably screwing his own sister-in-law."

They both laugh.

"Wow," Sharon says, and they laugh again.

Dick tells her a joke about a woman who goes to a psychiatrist because she has repeated dreams about long, pointed objects. "You know, like swords, pencils, arrows. 'That's very simple, dear lady,' the psychiatrist says. 'You are obsessed by phallic symbols.' 'By what?' the woman asks. 'By symbols of the phallus,' the psychiatrist tells her. 'Huh?' the woman says, and he can see she doesn't get it. He decides to do something really drastic. So, he gets up and opens his fly. 'There,' he says. '*That's* a phallus!' 'Ohhhh,' says the woman, 'like a penis, only smaller.'"

Neither of them laughs.

"I love Anna," Sharon says. "I really do."

"Me, too," Dick says. He stands, picks up his jacket and, leaning precariously over her, kisses her sweetly on the mouth.

After he leaves, Sharon feels restless and she lies awake for a long time. She thinks of an editor she knows who insists she remembers being born. She claims to have understood instantly her mother's profound sorrow at learning her baby was a girl.

Sharon thinks it's only hysteria induced by the editor's own disappointment in her life as a woman, and she argued that such early memory isn't possible, before language, before the ability to form concepts.

"Listen," the other woman said. "Dreaming begins *in utero.*"

What a notion—a tiny, crouched, and floating dreamer! The image has always appealed to Sharon, and thinking of it now, she floats, too, then starts to feel sleepy, the way Beau did whenever she wanted to talk in bed.

Floating. Once, when he was coming, Michael called out, "Oh, Sharon, your legs are holding me like arms!"

She meets Dick in the coffee shop for breakfast. "How do you feel?" he asks, and it is not a perfunctory question. He wants to know.

"Afraid of how I feel," Sharon answers. "Maybe more angry than sympathetic. Not loving enough, not *Christian.* Michael had such a rotten childhood, didn't he? I mean, his parents should have been arrested. It's a miracle that he's such a good person, really, isn't it? I'm like an evil-minded child in church, trying hard to have holy thoughts. And I feel so selfish now, as if the only crimes that matter are the ones committed against me."

She is exhausted, self-conscious. It was like a courtroom speech, or one made on a deathbed. "And I'm a little nauseous, besides," she adds.

Dick signals the waitress for the check.

At the car, he takes the driver's seat. Leaving the motor running, he gets out and goes into the motel office. When he comes back, he hands her a morning newspaper.

On the front page, there is a photograph of a baby who was born with his heart on the outside of his chest. Not the first recorded case, but still a medical phenomenon. Temporary surgical repair has been done to keep the baby alive until the cavity enlarges enough to hold the heart. Skin taken from his little legs and back has been used to build a thin wall against that terrible beating.

On the way to the jail, Sharon massages her cold hands and thinks about men and how they always wear their parts on the surface of their bodies, indecently exposed and vulnerable, appendages of their joy and their despair. She realizes that she has never regretted being female, as a girl or as a woman. If she were given another shot at it, she wouldn't choose a different animal form, either, not even a bird's with its feathered grace and alleged freedom. And she would never be a man for anything.

Except for the barred windows, the jail looks like a schoolhouse. There is a flag flapping outside, and on the corner a policeman, middle-aged and plump, like the friendly ones in children's primers, directs traffic.

They are taken to a room with a square table and four hard chairs in it. The door is left open, so that they hear the footsteps when a guard approaches with Michael, and she looks up and sees him immediately. He is attempting to smile, and about to weep.

Dick remains seated as Sharon stands and goes to Michael. When he puts his hands on her, she can feel the burning of his palms, and she goes into him, pressing the place where the flowers bloom.

(1979)

Mother

Despite what everyone said, Helen wasn't sure that she'd seen the baby. Maybe the ether had taken her memory of recent events or maybe she simply couldn't believe that anything this important had really happened to her. Ten years before, she'd been a spinster, working in a typing pool at a textile company and still living at home in Brooklyn with her father. How he must have pitied and despised her for having his broad, ruddy face, and such a sorry awkwardness in the world of men and women. It was to escape his sympathy that she'd gone to the dance that night and met Jon. Her father had come to the doorway of her room and caught her posing in the mirror, trying on her mother's crystal beads. When she saw him standing there, stout and pink in his uniform, she felt her face and throat blotch in that awful way. He smiled and said, "Going out tonight, Helen?" She'd had no intention of going anywhere. Nellie, another typist in the pool, had told her about a get-acquainted dance a single women's club was holding, to celebrate Warren G. Harding's election. Helen wasn't interested—she knew the political event was only an excuse for the social one, and she hated standing on the sidelines, wearing a frozen smile of expectation when she expected nothing. But she told her father that she was going out. "Just to a dance," she muttered.

"Well, that's nice, dear, that sounds like fun," he said. He touched his forehead, his chest, and his holster in a kind of nervous genuflection and pushed their hopeless conversation further. "Mother loved to dance in her heyday, you know," he said. He indicated the box of her mother's jewelry on the dresser. "Maybe you ought to wear some of that stuff . . . gussy up a little."

She pitied and hated him then, too, for pretending that twenty-eight was not a desperate age for a woman, that "gussying up" was the secret of fatal attraction, that he believed her capable of abandoned fun. Her mother had probably never danced. She'd probably never made love, either, with that great, aching hulk in the doorway. Maybe Helen had been born of some chaste, clothed act that produced only lesser beings. Her face blazed up again. Maybe she was going crazy at last, the way they said all lustful virgins eventually did. Her father continued to stand there, smiling.

The very worst thing, she was certain, was not human misery, but its nakedness, and the naked witness of others.

And as her father knew her hidden heart, so she knew his. She'd seen him standing for minutes in front of the open, smoking icebox, staring inside as if he expected something beyond butter or milk to be revealed. Then, with a heaving sigh, he always settled for butter and milk. His whole life had whizzed by like a bullet from the gun he'd never fired off the firing range, and here he was: long-widowed, still a foot patrolman, and with a sulky old-maid daughter on his hands. She'd inherited his homely looks, and out of spite she'd deny him his immortality. Her mother had died of pneumonia when Helen was two years old, and all she could recall were a few real or imagined impressions—breast, hair, shadow.

Lying in the maternity ward at Bellevue Hospital, Helen couldn't conjure up even the vaguest image of the living child they'd said she'd delivered. All the other women in her ward but one had infants at their breasts at regular intervals. The nurses wheeled them in in a common cart, like the vegetables sold by street peddlers. The woman in the bed opposite Helen's had given birth to a stillborn son. Before the wailing babies were distributed among the new mothers, a three-sided screen was arranged discreetly around her bed, and she could be heard weeping behind it.

Helen felt remote from the celebration around her, as she had felt remote from the festive possibilities of the dance the night she'd met Jon. The ballroom had been romantically lit for the occasion and adorned with political banners and posters. As soon as she walked in, she knew that her dress was wrong—she would disappear in the shadows. It was November and cold, and everyone, all the magazines, said that simple black was always smart and always right. Yet even Nellie and Irene, who lived by the dictates of fashion, wore gaily colored dresses and matching headbands. Oh, what difference did it make? There were so many women, in bright noisy clusters, and only a few men, aside from the band that was just warming up.

Irene glanced around and said, "Boy, I bet we'd find more fellas at a convent." She and Nellie leaned together, giggling. Helen didn't see what was so funny. They weren't beautiful or that popular, either, and the Great War had decreased all of their chances even further. But she was rallying to laugh along with them, to be a good sport, when the huge mirrored ball suspended from the center of the ceiling began to slowly revolve. Facets of light ricocheted off every surface and struck her painlessly on her arms, her dress, her shoes. The band started to play the lively melody of some popular song she couldn't name, but that she found herself humming. Everyone was wearing the same restless pattern of light. In that way they were all united, like jungle beasts marked by the spots or stripes of their species. Helen felt that something was about to happen. It was in the very air. Harding gazed down at her from the enormous posters like a stern but benevolent chaperone. And look, the ballroom was filling up—so many men were coming in! Irene said it was because *they* only had to pay half price, but who cared? Couples went whirling by in one another's arms. Before long, Nellie was pulled into the maelstrom, and a few minutes later Irene was gone, too. Soon someone would come for her, would know intuitively her concealed qualities: that she'd been golden blonde as a child, and her skin attested to it; that she had lovely breasts; that she could type sixty flawless words a minute.

A man seemed to be coming purposefully in her direction. She felt an immediate affinity with the gawkiness of his stride, the way his cowlick had resisted combing. He appeared hell-bent in his mission and an electric thrill traveled her body. Then she saw that he'd meant someone else, the gyrating flapper in fringed pink standing next to her, who shook her head no at him and turned to another man. Helen drew her breath in deeply and put up her arms, as if he'd meant her all along. He hesitated for the barest moment before he held out his own arms. She was careful not to lead.

They were married on Inauguration Day, and Jon moved in with Helen and her father. He was a typesetter for the *Sun*, with a modest salary. Their living arrangement enabled them to save money for the house they'd buy after they'd begun their own family. Helen stored their wedding gifts neatly in the walk-in cedar closet, so that everything would still be new no matter when they moved. The closet's cool, scented interior was like a little forest glade, and she often just stood there in a reverie, surrounded by the artifacts of her future.

Helen didn't become pregnant, though not for want of trying. Each disappointing month she wept in the privacy of the cedar closet, wiping her eyes carefully on the corner of one of the monogrammed wedding sheets. Old Dr. Kelly insisted she was fine, that nature would take its course, wait and see. When Helen asked if she should see a specialist, he laughed and shook his head. "Isn't the family doctor best when you want to start a family?" he said. "Didn't I deliver herself in my little black bag?"

Oh, yes, she thought, and took my mother away in it. He was like a gentle, cheerful priest, his undaunted cheer shaking her faith, but she gave him the wobbly smile he wanted. Finally, though, they did consult a specialist, in his Gramercy Park offices. She gasped during his examination and fainted during the first treatment to expand her fallopian tubes. He prescribed a nerve powder and told Jon that it was inadvisable for Helen to continue working in her condition.

She stayed home for two years, prowling the house like a high-strung watchdog. She'd left her job, but her fingers refused to give up typing. They tapped out imaginary letters about late shipments and damaged goods on the tabletops and the walls. She played game after game of patience, telling herself that if the next hand worked out, she would become pregnant that month. It was a relief to go back to work at last, to give up hope, if not the longing that had impelled it.

Helen and Jon developed the exclusive closeness of childless couples. After Helen's father died walking the orbit of his beat, they became even closer, insulated from the world of real families. Jon's parents and sisters were far away, on the farm in Minnesota he'd left years before. He and Helen had friends, of course, but their only important connection was to each other, a wondrous and scary thing. Once they'd stopped trying so hard to conceive, though, they made love less often, and it became more a matter of mutual comfort than a passionate pursuit.

When the Depression began, Jon's salary was cut in half and Helen lost her job, but they told themselves how lucky they were not to have to worry about anyone else during such difficult times. Helen took inordinate pride in her resourcefulness and her capacity for thrift. She made filling soups out of battered produce and scraps of meat, and screwed low-wattage light bulbs into all the lamps and fixtures. Going from door to door, she found various kinds of piecework they could do at home. She typed envelopes and stuffed them with flyers, and they both pasted glitter onto celluloid dolls. The stuff got into everything; it stuck to their fingers and was scattered in the carpets and on their clothing. At night, Helen saw a

trace of phosphorescent glitter on the pillows, like a
sprinkling of celestial dust. It reminded her of the fairy
tales her father had read to her years ago, in which worthy
wishes were granted and deprivation was ultimately
rewarded. The story she'd loved best was "The Goose
Girl," about a deposed princess who carried around a
cambric stained with three drops of her mother's blood.
Helen had always favored the most morbid stories: "The
Goose Girl" with its bloody cambric and decapitated
talking horse; "The Hardy Tin Soldier" melting away for
love and heroism; and, of course, "The Little Match
Girl." But even a happy ending couldn't dispel the essential melancholy of Grimm and Andersen. The goose girl
would lament, "Alas! dear Falada, there thou hangest,"
and the horse's head would answer, "Alas! Queen's
daughter, there thou gangest. If thy mother knew thy fate,
her heart would break with grief so great." Helen wasn't
quite sure what gangest meant, or cambric, for that matter,
but her own heart always broke on cue. Had she loved
those stories because she was a miserable child? Or had
they helped to make her that way?

When she did become pregnant, after ten years of
marriage, she decided never to read those stories to her
child. *Her child.* How remarkable that a living creature
could be made accidentally in darkness. That a reprieve
could come so long after the end of hope. Helen experienced bliss that seemed dangerous. Jon was as happy as she
was, although she knew he'd pretended acceptance of

their childlessness out of a kind of gallantry, just as he continued to pretend she was the girl he'd meant to dance with.

One morning, in Helen's seventh month of pregnancy, there were a few drops of blood on the sheet, and Dr. Kelly ordered her to bed. He came to examine her at home each week, and it was like being a child again—his minty, medicinal smell in the room, the black leather bag gaping on the dresser top. Sometimes, after he'd listened to her belly with his stethoscope, he would put it to her ears. What a marvelous din! It denied what she had feared most about herself, that she was inferior and unfinished, incapable of this simple biological purpose. She rested, reveling in daydreams, as she used to do in the cedar closet, and willed her body to wait out its sentence. It didn't, though.

Two weeks into her eighth month, she woke during the night with her waters flooding the bed. "Oh, Jesus," Jon said. "It's too soon!" While he went to fetch Dr. Kelly, their next-door neighbor came into their place in her nightgown. She worked dry blankets under Helen and crooned, "All right, dear. All right, all right."

It wasn't all right at all. Everything was happening so fast: the waters, and then the pain—accelerating, intensifying. The bed itself seemed to writhe. The neighbor crossed Helen's legs tightly and said, "Don't push! Lie still!"

Dr. Kelly came and he hoisted her from the bed, ordering Jon to take her feet and the other woman to carry his bag and throw the doors wide. They struggled down the stairs like barflies with a soused buddy, but they managed to get Helen to the street and into Dr. Kelly's car.

At Bellevue she was separated from Jon. The last thing she remembered of that night was his diminishing figure as she was wheeled down a hallway. When she woke, it was another day. Her mouth was sweet with ether and sour with sleep. They told her she'd had a daughter. They said that Jon had been to see her soon after, and that she'd spoken to him, but she didn't really remember that, either. She missed the baby in a physical way, with an emptiness that was not unlike hunger. Her breasts ached and leaked until a nurse came with a lethal-looking pump and expressed the milk. Helen was assured that the baby was alive, that this very milk would be fed to her soon in the nursery.

"Now you saw her, Helen," Dr. Kelly scolded, "just before we sent her down. You said she looked like a little drowned rat." And the nurse who gave her a sponge bath said, "Turn on your side for me now, Mother." They promised that she would be taken to the special nursery in the basement for another look as soon as she could tolerate a wheelchair ride. She'd lost a lot of blood, they told her, and she wasn't even ready yet to dangle her legs.

An aide propped Helen up for supper and she found herself facing the grieving woman, who sat immobile over her own tray. They looked at each other in the cheerful clamor of silverware. The woman's eyes returned Helen's commiseration, like a mirror, and her mouth twitched into a bitter, conspiratorial smile. Helen couldn't eat her supper. She was almost glad when the babies were brought in again, and the three-sided screen came between her and that knowing gaze.

That evening, Jon was in the herd of visitors who carried the chill of winter in on their clothes. Helen questioned him about the baby and he said that she was doing well, breathing nicely and taking nourishment. "What did Dr. Kelly say?" she asked. Jon glanced nervously away before he said, "He told me she's a little fighter, which makes all the difference." Helen knew that was only a partial truth, that the fate of premature infants was shaky, at best. They were meant to stay inside longer and develop. Their hearts and lungs might be too weak to sustain them, and they had no defenses against the slightest infection. She imagined the special nursery with its tiny, perishable occupants ticking away like homemade bombs.

"Well, what shall we name her, Helen?" Jon asked.

They had made up names, and even careers, for the unborn baby during those weeks in bed. They'd drawn up lists, under "Girl" and "Boy," but now she said, sullenly, "I don't know, I can't think about that now."

"They need it for the certificate," Jon said.

She had a sudden, dreadful image of the small, toppled tombstones in the old churchyard near their house. Some of them were over the graves of infants whose chiseled names and dates could still be read. "I don't want to name her yet," she said in a rising voice, and Jon quickly said, "All right, dearest, don't worry about it," which only made her feel worse.

He sat at her bedside, helpless against her mood. He held her hand and she was touched by the familiar sight of his ink-stained fingers. She thought of how he'd apologized for them the night of the dance, explaining that he'd come straight from work, that his hands weren't actually dirty. He'd worked so hard recently, and had never complained, even when she withdrew into the luxury of her interior life. Yet there were times he'd enraged her with that glance of mournful sympathy he might have learned from her father. Now she felt a swell of love for him at the same time that she felt impatience and a desire for him to go.

At last visiting hours were over, and Jon was ushered away with the other outsiders. In a while, the babies were brought in for their last feeding of the day. When they were taken out again, the overhead lights went off and a few of the bed lamps were switched on. Some of the women whispered together in the cozy dimness. Others combed their hair. This was the strangest hour, a time in the real world when only children are put to bed. Helen was very tired, but not sleepy. She couldn't find a comfortable position under the tight, starched sheets.

"Goodnight! Goodnight!" the happy mothers called to one another. One by one the lamps were shut off and the only visible light was outside the room at the nurses' station. The woman in the bed next to Helen's coughed and someone at the far end giggled. Someone else said, "Shhh!" Soon there was a refrain of slow, even breathing, the counterpoint of snoring. The shadow of the night nurse fell across the threshold as she stood and peered in at them.

After the nurse went back down the hall, Helen sat up and worked her way out of the sheets' bondage. She turned carefully on the high hospital bed and let her legs hang over the side. She became dizzy and had to sit still for a few moments. Then she slipped down until her feet were shocked by the cold floor. She found her slippers and stepped into them, and she put on her flannel robe. No one, not even the mother of the stillborn baby, stirred. Helen's bottom hurt and the thick sanitary pad she wore felt clumsy. She walked stiffly, sliding her feet along like someone learning to ice-skate. At the sink she paused and looked at herself in the mirror—an ashen wraith with glints of silver in its tousled hair, as if childbirth had aged her. She peered more closely and saw that it was only the celluloid dolls' glitter. She whispered "Mother" just to try it out, but it felt strange on her tongue, a foreign food for which she hadn't yet cultivated a taste. When she came to the doorway she stopped again, spent from so much exertion, and leaned against the frame. The nurses' station was empty, and there was nobody in the corridor.

It took a long time to walk the few yards to the stairway. Behind her the phone on the desk rang and rang. In the stairwell, Helen wondered what floor she was on. It didn't matter. They'd said the nursery was in the basement; she would go down and down until there were no more stairs. I've done this before, she thought, at the second or third landing, and then she knew it was school she was thinking of—the empty, echoing stairwell when she'd carried a note from one teacher to another while everyone else was in class. How privileged she'd felt, and free! But once she was punished in front of the whole assembly for talking when the flag was being carried in. She could never remember the joy without the shadow of humiliation. It was the danger of all happiness, and what she had willed to her mortal child. Alas, Queen's daughter.

There were two orderlies in the basement corridor, wheeling a squeaking gurney and laughing. Helen waited until they'd turned the corner, and then she shuffled out in the other direction. She smelled something cooking, the strong, beefy odor of institutional soup or gravy. It made her feel hungry and a little sick. She looked through the glass panel of one of the swinging doors that led to the kitchen. It was as brightly lit in there as the delivery room—she remembered *that* now, the impossible brilliance. She'd tried to say something about the stingy light they suffered at home, and then the mask had come down, dousing her voice and the lights at once.

In the kitchen, witches' cauldrons were bubbling on the giant stoves. Three women in hairnets chopped onions and wept, and an angry chef attacked a slab of meat. It was the landscape of nightmares, and here she was in her nightclothes, but awake. Feeling lightheaded, she went past the kitchen and at the corner of the corridor found a sign, its arrow pointing the way to the LABORATORY, X-RAY, and the MORGUE. The nursery had to be somewhere beyond them.

The locked laboratory door had a glass panel, too. There was no one inside; the feeble light might have been left on for the animals. She could see a few of them crouched in their cages: quivering brown rabbits, white rats squinting suspiciously back at her. She had surely never said that awful thing about the baby. It was only one of Dr. Kelly's silly bedside jokes. The rats scurried in their limited space and Helen shuddered and moved on.

There was no one in sight, and she longed to sit for a moment on one of the wooden benches on either side of the door to the X-ray room. But she was afraid that if she sat down, she'd be unable to get up again. Instead she slumped against the black door. It felt cold and solid. Years ago, when she was about thirteen, Helen developed a bad cough that Dr. Kelly's syrups and tonics couldn't cure. Her father took her to the clinic of one of the big uptown hospitals to have a picture taken of her chest. It was an unnerving procedure, and she could still recall the anxious darkness, and the icy pressure of the machine against her beginner breasts. After she was dressed, the doctor invited

Helen and her father into the consultation room, where
a backlit X-ray was hung. Astonished, she saw her own
tiny, lurking heart, and the delicate fan of ribs that housed
her lungs. With a pointer the doctor showed them a faint
shadow he said was a touch of wet pleurisy. Her father
was so relieved it wasn't pneumonia, he grasped the
doctor's hand, making him drop the pointer. Helen should
have been relieved, too, but she harbored a silent fury that
there could no longer be any secrets. Her father could
already read her evil thoughts, and now the last strong-
hold of privacy had fallen.

Later, she opened herself gladly to Jon, and then to the
baby. Leaning against the door to the X-ray room, she was
stirred by the memory of the child inside her, the thrill of
its quickening. "Push!" the nurse in the delivery room had
said, just as Helen's neighbor had ordered her not to push
when her labor first began. And then her body had made
its own willful choice. She could hear herself grunting,
those deep animal grunts of colossal effort. You were
never supposed to really remember the pain—that's what
all the women she knew had said. They'd told her it was
the worst pain in the world, and they said it with a kind
of religious fervor. But they promised that she'd forget it
afterward, as if it had all taken place in another life. Then
why was it coming back to her here in the basement
corridor, an echo of the pain and thrusting she'd believed
she could not survive? Then she remembered *everything*
that had happened under that dazzling sun: being shackled

to the table, the grunts changing to screams, the mask she'd risen to meet as if it were a lover's mouth. The missing part was still the birth itself—that happened in a long tunnel of dreamless sleep—and the baby. Where was the baby?

A child was crying somewhere, and Helen's breasts ran. The crying got louder and closer, and she slid along the wall to one of the benches and sat down. But it wasn't an infant's sound—these wails smothered language, and there were footsteps hurrying toward her. There was no place to hide, no time to even stand up. Two people, a man and a woman, half-carrying, half-dragging the shrieking child between them, turned the corner. Helen shrank against the bench in terror of being discovered.

The child banged his ear with his fist. The parents didn't seem to notice Helen's robe and slippers—the man shouted at her, "Where's the emergency room?" She was unable to answer him, although her mouth worked in spasms. They hurried past her, struggling with their struggling burden, their footsteps and the child's screams receding as they all disappeared at the next corner. God, she had wet herself! But when she looked down, she saw blood flowering her pink slippers and puddling the floor. She stood and stared in amazement. The child with the earache still screamed in the far distance.

"Help me," Helen said. "Help me!" she said, louder. Of course no one responded; she had to get back to the kitchen where there were people. She stood there in confusion before she was able to push off. Then it was as if the walls moved past her, and she walked on a treadmill. She was on fire, she was melting. "Papa," she whimpered. "Jon!" When she came to the morgue, she knew she had gone in the wrong direction. Her fists were soft against the door and they tingled with pins and needles, as if she had just woken and had to wait for them to wake, too. She thought she heard someone in there, or a radio playing, but she might have been hearing noises inside her own head. She was afraid to look at her slippers now, and she was shivering with cold. "*Please*," she said, and turned to follow the drunken, slithery trail of blood. The first of it on and near the bench had already started to darken. It looked like the remains of an accident after the victims have been carted away.

She staggered past the bench and went like a moth to the lighted window of the laboratory. The rats looked back at her. She gasped, as she had gasped during the last earthshaking pain of her waking labor. When she'd emerged from the tunnel she saw the glistening blue-pink baby hung by its feet, girdled by the thick, pulsing cord. "Oh!" she had cried. "Oh! It looks like a little drowned rat!" That wasn't what she'd meant to say. She'd meant words of welcome and consolation for the terrible gift of the world. There thou gangest.

She fell through the double doors of the kitchen and saw the three women and the chef in a sudden, frozen tableau. She came to once more, somewhere else, with Dr. Kelly looming over her saying, "No! Oh, Christ, damn it!" Then she felt her soul folding end on end on end, like the flag from her father's coffin, like the wedding sheets in the cedar closet, until it was small enough to slip through the open mouth of the waiting black leather bag.

(1987)

Love

The way it was, I didn't love anybody. Not even Ezra. I looked down at him in his bath, dispassionate about the soft pink hills of his knees rising from the silvered water.

I don't love you, kiddo, I thought, and I poured shampoo into the whorl of hair on top of his head. Maybe I could have loved a more conventional child, aptly named Scott or Michael or Andrew, a boy without Ezra's wheezing allergies, without his straight and penetrating glance. The average American boy, I thought, *drops* his eyes when you look at him, and so prepares for the evasiveness he will use when he grows up and screws around.

I didn't really love Gene then, either. I was possessive of him, I was manic; I wouldn't give him up to Bonnie or anyone. But it was hard to concentrate on *love*, on the energy it required. Fuck love, I thought, and I smiled at my own ingenuity. Ezra smiled back at me.

"Head down, sweetheart," I said firmly and he ducked, docile and sweet. The shampoo beaded up and frothed into perfect opals that slid down behind his ears. Maybe they should come up with a new shampoo for kids like Ezra, something potent and authoritative named Fist or Hard-On or War. Instead his scalp was rosy and clean from Breck for Normal or Dry Hair.

After Ezra's bath we went into the kitchen and I washed the breakfast dishes while he drew pictures in an old notebook. Only yesterday Gene had left, off to Bonnie's for good (for bad, I thought), and here I was today busy with ordinary chores. Scouring powder drifted down into the sink like blue snow. I went into the bedroom and dialed Bonnie's number. They must have been waiting all night for permission or a benediction, because she picked up the phone after the first ring and exhaled loudly into my ear. "Hello. Hello!"

"Listen," Gene had said last night. "It's no good being like this." He meant crazy, and he wouldn't dare look at my crazy eyes and my bubbling mouth. "Come to your senses," he ordered. "Call me when you come to your senses."

"*Hello*," Bonnie insisted, and I hung up. I was entitled to erratic behavior. Nobody could begrudge me that.

When Ezra was dressed we went downstairs and walked to the corner. We took the crosstown bus to Dr. Freedman's office on the East Side. Because this was Ezra's domain he took over, greeting Arlette, the pretty receptionist, then gathering a lapful of worn and familiar Golden Books. I sat in my overcoat, feeling transient and sad. I picked up a copy of *Today's Health* and read a long article on contact dermatitis. God, the world was full of pitfalls. Ezra usually went in accompanied by Arlette for his shots and his five-minute chat with Dr. Freedman, who was psychologically oriented. What did they talk about in there? How did they communicate? Where was the middle ground between *Wonderama* and the supple thighs of Dr. Freedman's receptionist? I never asked Ezra. I knew instinctively that you don't ask a boy what he says to his allergist. In turn Dr. Freedman never accused me of making Ezra wheeze. Today I would have liked a crack at him myself. I would have asked him point-blank, "Which is better for an allergic child, a dust-free broken home and a step-mother young enough to be called Bonnie or a house-hold held together with spit?" Ezra went in, holding hands with Arlette, and I sat and waited like a backstage mother.

When Ezra was finished we took another bus, uptown this time and into a neighborhood that was no longer expensive. It was considered a dangerous neighborhood, too, where my mother and grandmother lived, and I whistled and sang to warn off muggers and rapists, and the kidnappers of my childhood fantasies.

"Who? Who is it?" my mother wanted to know. She came into the kitchen, her bleached hair in wet, pinned scrolls against her head. Her fingers were splayed, held in front of her so that the polish would dry safely, yet it seemed as if she were bestowing a blessing. My grandmother had let us in, the smoke of her cigarette churning through her nostrils. "The color is good, Frances. Nice and even." It was Saturday and they had touched up each other's hair. They sat down together at the kitchen table, crowned in identical gold. "MMM-wah!" They both made smacking sounds with their lips at Ezra. They would hug him when their nails were dry.

"Sugar doll," my mother crooned.

"Lover man," said my grandmother. They waved their hands in the air and blew on their nails.

"Am I drying dark?" my mother asked.

"No, Frances, no. It's a good shade. You look wonderful. Some lucky guy should take a look at you."

"Oh, Ma," she said happily. Because my mother didn't need a man at all. All of her love was played out years ago and she just didn't have the vigor for the real thing anymore. When the butcher teased her and called her Honeybunch, when a dopey teenager in the building gifted her with a frozen Milky Way, she was satisfied. The fictional sex lives of famous people were as real and gratifying as a warm man under the sheets with her. Real, unreal, it was all the same. She said that my father had reddish hair, yet in his picture it seemed to be dark. My God, I thought, this would make three generations of us.

My father was long gone, having left us in another neighborhood I could hardly remember. And I could hardly remember him. It was difficult to separate memory from what I had been told by my mother, that unreliable narrator. Was my father light- or dark-haired? He was very tall, she insisted, yet in the picture they seem to be standing eye to eye. They met nine months before I was born. It was at a roller-skating rink and the voice on the loudspeaker called for mixed couples in a waltz number. And from that carefree act of a boy and a girl dancing on wheels to "The Blue Danube," their chests swelling with the rise of the organ music, came all those unexpected effects. My grandmother, me, an apartment with its domestic trappings and snares. He ran and never came back.

I thought I would tell them about Gene. I might even have a temper tantrum here in their pink and white kitchen. After all, if blame is to be cast, you can't go back too far. Had they groomed me to be a discarded woman?

A shower of soft gray ashes fell into my grandmother's lap. She gave Ezra a dish of orange Jell-O, scraping the rubbery edges off with a knife. What if they gave me advice? They might say, Don't be a dope, Sandy. Don't let him get away with it. It's all hot pants anyway. Or they might say, Let him go good riddance to bad rubbish come and live with us and on Saturday we will gild your hair and shave your legs.

Ezra sucked at his Jell-O.

My mother speculated about how Dean Martin's and Frank Sinatra's children really feel about their fathers. I wondered where my father was at that very moment. I wondered if he ever went roller-skating again. I wondered if Gene and Bonnie were undressed together right then and how she observed his body and if she could appreciate it without having witnessed its changes. Bonnie is small and round. She is young and sweet like a babysitter or a nurse or a waitress in a cocktail lounge.

"I don't care," my mother said. "I wish *I* was Nancy Sinatra."

"Ah, you're a crazy mixed-up kid," my grandmother told her. She smashed out her cigarette in an El Morocco ashtray.

They cuddled Ezra. Allergic children need a great deal of cuddling. My mother gave him a quarter. My grandmother gave him thirty-two cents. The pennies kept rolling out of his hands as they kissed him. They sent their love to Gene and they blew kisses from the doorway. Then they went inside to comb each other out. All the way down the stairs I kept silent, daring whoever was waiting, but my defiance must have been felt and we passed through unharmed.

We stopped at a luncheonette on the way home and we shared a cheese sandwich and a soda. I bought a wooden backscratcher with a hand carved at the end of it, for Ezra. He raked it against my arm and I forced a toothy smile at him. I went into the phone booth and dialed Bonnie's number. This time Gene answered and I felt a mild vertigo at the sound of his voice. I breathed, my breath like Ezra's when he is near a shedding dog, "Huh, huh," my breath said.

"Oh, I know it's you," he said, as kind and righteous as Perry Mason. "Listen, it's not the end of the world. We have to take care of certain things. We have to talk about them. Are you home now? Will you *answer* me? For Christ's sake, Sandy. It's a weapon, Sandy."

"Huh, huh." I couldn't stop that damn breathing. I looked back through the glass at Ezra who sat at the counter stroking himself with the backscratcher. His eyes were closed and his lips were open. He was giving himself pleasure. In my ear the operator whispered that my time was up and, obedient, I replaced the receiver.

When we came to our apartment the phone was ringing. A silent conspiracy existed between Ezra and me. He didn't run to answer the phone and I didn't tell him not to. We sat down together in the living room. Ezra stroked his backscratcher against the yellow velvet of his chair. It left long track marks in the fabric. "Do you know what Dr. Freedman said?" he asked.

I sat up, alerted, out of my slouch. "Hmm?" I said, nondirective.

"He said he loves me."

Loves him! What a phony creep! I felt disappointed, sick at heart.

"*Everybody* loves you," I told him.

The weight of this news made Ezra sigh deeply. "But not everybody knows me," he said.

In a little while he went to sleep and I went back into the living room. I tried to read a book, but tears came to my eyes, magnifying the words, making them run off the page. I went into the bedroom and took off all my clothes. Generous to myself, I lit only a dim, pink-shaded lamp. I stood in front of the mirror. My body is nice, everything holding up well and the skin silky and firm. It is such a familiar body, the mole under the left breast exactly where I remembered it. I looked at myself with loyalty and affection. And yet I had to be honest. Here and there were signs that couldn't be ignored. Undefined blue shadows behind the knees. The flesh in the midriff came together too easily between my fingers. I looked at it sadly as I might at a favorite dress that had not given full service.

I lay down on the bed, thinking I could probably seduce him if he were there in that same room, in that same bed, seeing those familiar blurred images through his eyelashes as he turned to me. How could he do without me? How could this happen?

I jumped up and went into Ezra's room. He was asleep, his arms out, his breath soft and perfect. I took the back-scratcher from the floor near his shoes and went back to my bed. I pulled the long wooden handle along one leg and then the other. Slowly, I scratched at my arms, up and down in that same gentle rhythm. And I willed Gene to the bedside, pulling him there. He came, but I had conjured him up with his hands in his pockets and his shoulders hunched. He wouldn't look at me or sit in the inviting well of sheets and blankets. Instead, he stood at the window and looked out. "I wish the damn weather would change. It's always the same." He picked up a magazine. "Could you wear your hair this way? Do you think you'd like another climate?"

Here, I said. Over here.

But he wishes that he had finished graduate school. He wishes that he could stop smoking, that he had been different with his mother and father. His shoulders still hunched, he paces the floor, and it grieves me to watch him. So I roll over, starting on my back, keeping time with his footsteps. I satisfy one place, arouse another, and I know nothing will do any good. Nothing will stop him in the whole world.

I sat up and pulled the backscratcher across my chest and I saw the pink line of the scratch fade and then rise in the pallor of a welt. It was as if I had pierced through to the heart itself.

I put on my bathrobe and went to the telephone. Bonnie answered and her voice was tired. "Let me speak to him," I said, and Gene said, "Hello. Would you just listen for once? Don't you know I don't want to hurt you or the kid—God, it's awful." And he began to cry.

I said, "It's all right. I've come to my senses."

(1971)

The Great Escape

I used to look at Howard first thing in the morning to see if he was awake, too, and if he wanted to get something going before one of the kids crashed into the room and plopped down between us like an Amish bundling board. Lately, though, with the children long grown and gone to their own marriage beds, I found myself glancing over to see if Howard was still alive, holding my breath while I watched for the shallow rise and fall of his, the way I had once watched for a promising rise in the bedclothes.

Whenever I saw that he was breathing and that the weather waited just behind the blinds to be let in, I felt an irrational surge of happiness. Another day! And then another and another and another. Breakfast, vitamins, bills, argument, blood pressure pills, lunch, doctor, cholesterol medicine, the telephone, supper, TV, sleeping pills, sleep, waking. It seemed as if it would all go on forever in that exquisitely boring and beautiful way. But of course it wouldn't; everyone knows that.

There were running death jokes in our family. My father, driving past a cemetery: "Everybody's dying to get in." My mother: "Death must be great—nobody ever comes back." Howard's mother: "When one of us dies, I'm going to Florida." That would have been funny except that she actually meant it. Now, none of them was laughing or ever coming back.

Howard's father, who had no apparent sense of humor, was the first to go, quickly, of a blood clot that stopped his heart like a bullet. This sent Howard right to the precipice without fair warning. *Next!* He seemed to be summoned as if he'd been waiting his turn at the deli counter. He even told me that his number was up, extending the metaphor.

He wasn't next, though. His pushy mother cut the line and went second, succumbing to kidney failure after a short, spirited stint as the Merry Widow of Boca Raton. Then my parents sailed off into the abyss, felled in tandem by dementia and a series of strokes. We'd had our own health scares—Howard's enlarged prostate, a lump in my breast. Several of our friends beat us to it anyway, in a kind of social massacre, while, in what seemed like only a few long afternoons, he and I turned seventy and then eighty and then nearly ninety.

We had been together for such a long time that all of our grievances had been set aside, if not completely forgotten. Every once in a while, out of nowhere, I would remember his infidelities with a startling sting. And he must have still harbored resentment about what he'd called my "martyrdom," my "too-muchness," which, in truth, was only my largesse, my gregarious, forgiving nature.

But the business of being old took up most of our time and concentration. A schedule for our various pills and tonics was stuck by a magnet to the refrigerator, where we used to hang the children's drawings, then the grand-children's. And our bodies let us down as we lurched toward oblivion. My statuesque figure had given way to random bulges, as if my curves had been rearranged by an inept or sadistic sculptor. "Good padding against a hip fracture," Dr. Ginsberg said in dubious consolation. Then there was the matter of my heart. There was nothing really wrong with it, but I was often uncomfortably aware of its beating, like the meter ticking in a taxi stuck in traffic.

Howard, who had once been so gorgeous and in such hot demand, was grizzled and paunchy and gray. He couldn't quite believe what had happened to him, and he avoided mirrors and what he perceived as the pitying glances of strangers. I didn't tell him that I still had images of his younger self in the strongbox of my brain, of both of us at the beginning, when we couldn't keep our hands off each other. My nostalgia would be cold comfort for his sense of loss. I wondered if he remem-bered us, too, but I was too afraid, or shy, to ask.

I often said that we were lucky to still be alive, but he had to know I was lying. This hurt and that. "What?" one of us yelled to the other from the next room. "What is it now?" The little flash fires of frustration and anger. We'd both become relief maps of keratoses, skin tags, and suspicious-looking moles. "What's this thing on my back, Paulie?" Howard would say, yanking up his shirt while I searched for my reading glasses. "It's nothing," I'd tell him. "I have a million of those." Cheerleader and competitor at once. And I finally understood why my father, in his dotage, kept going on about his feet.

The children telephoned, Ann far more regularly than Jason, of course. She was the good, attentive child, the one with keys to our apartment—"just in case"—and with our super's and Dr. Ginsberg's numbers on her speed dial. "Mom," she would say without so much as the preface of a hello. "Are you okay? Is Dad?" As if she had heard we'd been in a terrible car accident, when neither of us even drove anymore.

Then she would relay a spate of news—world news first, in a flurry of headlines: the latest chaos at the White House, a terrorist attack in London or Boston or Beirut, another police shooting of an unarmed Black man, and did I know that someone famous had just died? Howard and I read the *Times* every day and watched CNN after supper, but Ann seemed to hear about everything first. I think she received bulletins on her watch or somewhere. Personal news usually followed, from the mundane—she thought she was getting a cold, and her brother had asked to borrow money again, for weed probably—to the spectacular: She'd made partner at her law firm! Her daughter Abigail was three months pregnant! Ann and Bradley were going to be grandparents. When I broke this latest to Howard he burst into tears. I put my arms around him and wept, too. And then we laughed together. How joyful we were, and how astounded that we had come to this.

Ann and I conspired on a daily basis about possible baby names, as if we'd have a say on the subject. It was going to be a boy; what would sound euphonious with Leff-Bernstein, Abigail and her husband, Greg's, conjoined last names? Jeremy? Dominic? Leo? Howard wondered if the baby might be named for him—after he was dead, that is, in the Jewish tradition. "Shut up," I told him. Why did he always have to spoil things?

I offered to host a baby shower and Ann agreed, although she insisted, in her amiably bossy way, that it would be held at her spacious SoHo loft instead of my junior four in Washington Heights, and that she would choose the theme and the caterer and cover all of the expenses. Which left me as no more than an honorary hostess, but I didn't argue with any of it. At a certain point, you have to accept the shift in the balance of power

between you and your children. And it was just so good
to have something to look forward to.

Then one wintry day Ann called very early in the morning.
Howard and I were still eating breakfast. "Listen, Mom,"
she said. "There's something going around, a virus."

"I read something about that in the *Times*. I hope it's
not like SARS or that other one . . . MERS?" When had
these dire uppercase acronyms slipped into our vocabulary? With AIDS, I remembered.

"It's in the same family," Ann said, "and it may be
very contagious. You and Dad should be careful."

"Well, we're not kissing anybody." Not even each
other, I didn't add.

"You should both stay close to home for now," Ann
said.

"We don't go anywhere," I said, "beside Safeway and
the doctor." I needed a haircut, though, my book club was
scheduled to meet soon—we were reading *Mrs. Bridge*—
and Howard wanted to get to the podiatrist to have his
toenails clipped as soon as Medicare would allow it.
Feet.

"Order in for now," Ann advised. "I can set you up
with a good food service. And cancel everything else."

"Sweetheart," I said. "Aren't you being a little
extreme?"

"Mother. I have it on good authority."

She probably did. Ann was on the board of two hospitals, with privileged access to several noted specialists.

"Well, what's it called? Maybe I'll ask Ginsberg about it."

She sighed. "*Ginsberg*," she said.

She had never exactly called Dr. Ginsberg a quack, but she'd intimated that he wasn't up to her high standards. I pointed out that Howard and I had survived almost half a century in his care, and that he always returned phone calls, usually the same day. I didn't say that I was a little bit in love with him, and that her father might be, too.

"It's called novel coronavirus," Ann said.

"Sounds fictional," I quipped, but she didn't laugh.

"The word 'novel' refers to the fact that it's new, unknown," she said, "which is what makes it so worrisome."

Later, I reported what Ann had told me about the virus to Howard, and he said, "I think she's becoming a bit of a hypochondriac."

"Gee, I wonder where she got that," I said. How many times had I caught him surreptitiously taking his pulse or his temperature?

"Ha ha," he said without a trace of mirth.

"Maybe we should listen to her. She's always up on everything, and she's so well-connected."

"Whatever," Howard said. "But I'm making an appointment with Perez. I can hang from a tree by my toenails."

I'll remember that exchange forever, although I barely registered it at the time. How strange the human mind is.

When my mother began to lose hers, she tried not to acknowledge it and I was her willing accomplice. "Everyone forgets a few words," she said after such a long mid-sentence pause on the phone I thought we'd been disconnected. It wasn't an unreasonable claim. Howard and I already suffered from an occasional folie-à-deux forgetfulness—unable to come up with Ida Lupino's name while we were watching one of her movies, or what the brussels sprouts on our dinner plates were called. But my mother's harmless "senior moments" devolved into some bizarre behavior. Either that or my father was the one losing it when he called to report that she'd been chewing on Kleenex or that she'd tipped the handyman in their building a hundred dollars for changing a ceiling lightbulb.

So I found myself sitting in her Elmhurst living room, with its battling floral patterns of wallpaper and upholstery, smiling falsely while sneaking glances at the Kleenex box on the end table closest to her. Two brazen cockroaches skittered across the middle of the floor in plain view. Usually, she'd be screaming at my father to take off his shoe and kill them, although he invariably missed his target and knocked over a lamp or stubbed his toe in the process. But this time she didn't seem to notice, and I think he pretended he didn't, either.

Yet she looked all right—her housedress was clean and buttoned correctly, and her conversation was ordinary enough. She offered me the requisite repulsive snacks of canned peaches and lime Jell-O. She asked after Howard and the kids, getting everyone's name right without hesitation. She said, "Your father is driving me crazy"—a familiar refrain—before ticking off a list of his latest crimes: he dropped crumbs everywhere, he loaded the dishwasher with the knives facing up, he added salt to his food without even tasting it. *Your father,* as if *I* was the one who had brought him into the family. Then, "Do you like your hair like that, Paulette?" Her customary, sly way of criticizing me, of telling the truth slant. But all of those maddening old habits of hers only elicited a whoosh of relief and even a ripple of affection. I was beginning to relax when she reached over and pulled a Kleenex from the box near her elbow and popped it into her mouth.

"Stock up on toilet paper and hand sanitizer," Ann advised. "Fill up your freezer."

By then, the virus had spread a little. "Annie," I said, it's not here. Some guy went to China, and now it's in Seattle. It's in a nursing home there." Where there were other, more decrepit and less fortunate old people, thousands of miles away. It was in the paper, and on the nightly news. Anderson Cooper seemed calmer than my daughter.

"Do you want to die, Mom?" she asked.

"Hmm. Good question."

"Stop it," she said. Then, "Don't you remember when you promised me that you would never die?"

She was three or four at the time, and had just had her first intimations of mortality after the death of her goldfish. It was an easy leap from Goldie to me, and she was inconsolable; what else could I say? "I never said that," I told her, blithely erasing her memory. "I said that I wouldn't die until you were ready for me to."

"I don't remember that," she said. "But anyway, I'm not ready. So don't." Her voice had thickened a little.

My poor girl. I didn't remind her of the message I'd once found scribbled with a marker inside the cover of the board game Sorry. *I hope Mommy dies.* At first I suspected Jason, who was given to that kind of sentiment in some of his adolescent outbursts, but it was clearly Ann's writing, down to the incongruous little heart dotting the *i*. She'd probably written it after a contentious family round of the game; she was never a gracious loser.

"Okay," I agreed. "I won't die yet."

Harry Houdini and his wife, Bess, famously made a pact to try and establish contact after one of them died. They came up with secret code words and other private signals and signs. He died first, and she held regular séances on his birthday for a decade, attempting to coax Harry's spirit into communicating. She failed, of course. My mother got that right—death is great; nobody ever comes back, or sends messages from the other side.

One night, in bed, just after Howard and I had taken our Ambien and turned off our lamps, I said, "If we made a deathbed pact, like the Houdinis', what would our secret code be?"

Howard groaned. "Jesus," he said. "Let's just go to sleep." Death was his least favorite topic, in any context, and especially at bedtime. So I didn't share my conviction that there was only one mystery left after a lengthy marriage: Which partner would die first? And I had stopped reminding him to check those blank boxes on his living will about heroic measures, about the withholding of food and water. He wasn't amused when I'd threatened him with an Incomplete.

The bed creaked now with his restless displeasure. "Why do you always have to talk about everything?" he said. A fair, if rhetorical, question. Why, indeed? Why did I feel compelled, as a small child, during a lull in the chanting at a family seder, to announce loudly that I had a vagina? Why did I tell Howard that I loved him before he had a chance to say it to me first? Did I think that "I love you," and "I love fucking you" were the same thing?

" 'To sleep, perchance to dream,' " I said, relentlessly. Hamlet's take on dying. "Remember when that idiot hotel in LA put those cards with the quote on our pillows?"

I could sense Howard smiling in the darkness. "Next to the mints," he said. Then, after a moment or two, "They called Houdini the Handcuff King."

"Sounds kinky," I said. But I felt sad. Harry and Bess—like the Trumans, like someone's old uncle and aunt in the Bronx, longing for each other from the grave. "So what would our secret code be?"

Howard didn't answer and I thought he'd fallen asleep. He sometimes did that in the middle of a conversation, a gift I believed was exclusively granted to men. But then he pulled me to him and kissed me deeply. I kissed him back—so hard our teeth collided—and his hand grazed one of my breasts and then the other. How lonely I had been for his touch, for his mouth. We did whatever we could still do to satisfy our resurgent desire, and we stayed in each other's arms afterward. I was just dozing off when Howard said, "Paulie."

"Yes?"

"That's my code word," he said. "Go back to sleep."

By early March there were a few cases in New York City. I didn't need Ann to tell me about them, although she'd already sent us a care package of surgical masks and vinyl gloves. Howard put on a mask and growled, "I've got a gun. Give me all your dough."

Then, in the middle of a weekday, there was a surprise visit from our son, Jason. He was between jobs—he'd been a bartender, an appliance salesman, and a greeter at a Walmart until they phased the position out. Decades ago, Howard had taken him on as an apprentice at his music studio, but Jason was often late getting in, and he kept screwing up. "I'm sorry, Dad," he said, finally. "It's just not my bag."

"He'll find himself, Howie," I predicted, I promised.

"I don't think he's even looking," Howard said.

Now Jason might be between marriages, too. I loved his current, second wife, Honey, the antithesis of the evil stepmother to his daughter, Summer. They'd separated before, and I kept hoping they would resolve things and become a couple again. For the time being he was couch surfing with friends on the Lower East Side.

"Just checking up on you guys," he said, handing me a bunch of bright green carnations. Was it St. Patrick's Day already, without a parade?

"You look like a bum," Howard told him after they'd hugged. Such a handsome bum, I thought, even in his sixties—we'd all be on Medicare together soon—with his father's dark eyes, and that stubble. He had been a mere comma under my ribs at our shotgun wedding, and now he filled the doorway. Like a mother in a sitcom, I tousled his hair and made him lunch. Before he left, Howard slipped him a twenty.

★ ★ ★

"And you let that moron into the apartment?" Ann shrieked over the phone. "I'll bet he took the subway there!" No, he took a limousine, a chariot, a flying carpet.

"Did you wear your masks, at least? Did you wash your hands?"

"Yes," I lied. I was getting better and better at it. "Of course we did."

It was my friend Ruth's turn to host our book group, but on the advice of her son Jeffrey, a radiologist, she called everyone to cancel, or at least to change the venue. We were going to have a Zoom meeting, whatever that was, instead of convening at her place. There was much nervous back and forth among the members of the group about this latest development. Everyone had a computer or an iPad, but there was a wide range of technical expertise. It sounded easy enough, though. We'd all receive a link and, at the specified time, we would simply open it and go from there.

Ours was strictly a women's group, and the few husbands still around were usually banned from our meetings. Whenever it was my turn, I took my laptop into the living room, where the refreshments were laid out, and Howard skulked off to the bedroom like a grounded teenager, closing the door behind him.

But the Zoom meeting changed all of that. Enough aloneness! We had to stick together. Ruth, long a widow, would have Jeffrey right beside her to help facilitate things, and I invited Howard to sit next to me on the bed, with the laptop between us. I hit the link and we waited, the way our ancestors must have waited for the flickering Magic Lantern to do its thing. After what seemed like a long time, the screen filled with a notice that our meeting would begin soon. "Well, this is exciting," I said.

Mrs. Bridge was my favorite novel, with its brief, brilliant paragraphs like vaudeville blackouts, and characters I would think about wistfully, as if they were old friends with whom I'd lost touch. I loved Mrs. Bridge, even when she exasperated me. She was the product of her circumstances, of her time and place, but I still wanted her to have more insight and more courage, and to make better choices, the way I had once wished for a happier outcome for Emma Bovary and Anna Karenina. When I was very young, I'd read a beloved book over and over again with the stupid hope that it would end differently this time. A few critics had said, when *Mrs. Bridge* and its sequel, *Mr. Bridge*, were first published, that they were unkind, even brutal portraits of the author's parents, whose upper middle class lives in Kansas City bore a strong resemblance to his protagonists'. But I saw both novels as candid observation, leavened by the charity of humor and the imagination. I was gripping my dog-eared, underlined book and looking forward to saying some of all that when our meeting began, if it ever did.

Suddenly, Ruth's and Jeffrey's faces loomed before us, almost as big as life. They were both wearing the kind of masks Ann said you couldn't buy anymore for love or money. Then one of them seemed to bark, piercingly, and Jeffrey shouted "Mute, Evelyn, mute!" Evelyn Lasky and Mildred, her ancient, incontinent, and yappy Maltese.

"How?" Evelyn cried. "Oh! Oh! What do I do?" while Mildred barked in frantic unison.

"Just hit your damn mute button!" Jeffrey commanded through his mask, as muffled and menacing as Darth Vader. "And shut that dog up!" So much for his bedside manner, I thought, but didn't say. What if I wasn't muted, either?

Then, the faces of all the other women in our book group popped up, each in a separate little frame, like the celebrities on *Hollywood Squares*. Some of the women's mouths were moving soundlessly. Only Evelyn's frame was empty until she whizzed by, calling "Mildred! Stay! Come!"

"Everyone else, unmute!" Jeffrey ordered, and soon there was a cacophony of voices, a chorus of confusion and dismay. And someone's cell phone chirped and chirped.

"So this is what I've been missing all these years," Howard said.

Then Ruth was in the center of the screen again, sans Jeffrey, holding up her copy of *Mrs. Bridge* and wiggling it. "Settle down, people," she said, like the middle school teacher she had once been. "Now, who would like to begin?"

I raised my hand and leaned eagerly forward—the way I had in AP English—just as the connection was broken and everyone grew silent and disappeared.

The sirens woke me again from a disturbing dream. Out of the frying pan . . . Howard was still asleep next to me, still breathing. Everything had changed in just a couple of weeks. There were so many new cases in the city and not only in nursing homes. I remembered telling Ann that I wouldn't be caught dead in one of those places.

Novel coronavirus, Covid-19—like the devil, it had alternate names. A neighbor informed me, through her barely cracked door, that someone on the floor below us had it, and there were rumors about the super's wife. Howard stayed home most of the time, pacing the apartment for exercise like a hamster on a wheel. I only ventured out for a few essentials at a small bodega rather than the more treacherously populated supermarket, and to pick up the mail and empty our trash. I wore a mask and gloves like almost everyone else I saw in the street. We all looked like aliens, like expressionless robots. One afternoon, I saw a barefaced young man coming toward me and I said, "Excuse me, but don't you have a mask?"

"Cunt!" he shouted, and he lunged at me with a raised fist before sauntering off. *Why do you always have to talk about everything?* My heart rioted for minutes afterward.

Upstairs, the phone rang and rang. An automated voice offered a terrific deal on automobile insurance. I just had to press "one" to reach an agent. Another told me that my Amazon account had been hacked and that I owed $1,046. A sweet-sounding boy pretended to be my grandson who needed Target gift cards sent immediately to bail him out of jail. I guess they all figured we were trapped at home and had nothing else to do, which was largely true.

But there also were legitimate, welcome calls, from both children, a couple of the grandkids, and our daughter-in-law, Honey. She was taking Jason back in, for the duration, anyway; she didn't want him to be among strangers in a plague.

"Darling," I said. "That sounds almost biblical."

"I guess I'm just a sucker, like you," she said, which felt absurdly like a compliment.

Rosa, who had been our weekly housecleaner for years, phoned to say she wouldn't be coming in for a while, or working for any of her other regulars. She was afraid of bringing something bad home to her disabled husband and his elderly mother, who lived with them. How would they get by without Rosa's income? I put some money in an envelope and mailed it to her, the way my mother used to send a crisp ten-dollar bill to Jason and Ann on each of their birthdays. I dragged the vacuum cleaner out of the hall closet. It seemed to draw back, like an obstinate leashed dog. I was embarrassed to realize I'd forgotten how to turn it on.

Houdini—that escape artist, the Handcuff King—was a great magician, but also a pragmatist. He knew that his tricks were just that, not anything mystical or otherworldly. So why did he and Bess ever devise that ridiculous pact? Maybe terror makes believers of us all.

Howard hated wearing a mask. He claimed that it impeded his breathing and, perversely, his vision. At the same time, he'd become more of a germaphobe, not touching the mail or the newspaper until they'd lain around the apartment for hours, and then washing his hands raw. Every few days he developed a new imaginary symptom, usually shortly after he'd first heard about it. One evening I found him sniffing an almost full bag of garbage—coffee grounds and onion peels—as if he were inhaling the scent of roses. "I think I've lost my sense of smell," he said. I opened an old jar of Vicks VapoRub and held it under his nose, and he recoiled, relieving us both.

I'd taken to reading aloud again, which used to annoy him, especially if he was trying to read at the same time.

Now, he seemed to find it soothing, maybe because I chose poems by Lucille Clifton and Billy Collins that tended to remind us of ourselves.

I didn't get my hair cut and it grew at what seemed to be an accelerated pace. There was nothing more unattractive, I thought, than an old woman with long, scraggly gray hair. I found a purple scrunchie that Abigail or Summer had left at our place and pulled my hair into a makeshift ponytail that made my ears stick out. Howard said he liked the way I looked. I wasn't the only liar in the family. He put on a CD of Sidney Bechet standards and we slow-danced around the living room for a few laps before collapsing together on the sofa. We'll get through this, I thought.

Then Howard told me that he had an ingrown toenail—it was killing him—and he'd made an appointment to see Dr. Perez.

"Let me see it," I said. "Maybe I can fix it." I had been filing my own toenails with a coarse emery board.

"You're not a podiatrist," he said.

"No," I said. "But I play one on TV."

He was not in a playful mood. His toe wasn't killing him, exactly—he was given to hyperbole—but it hurt a lot. "Howie, you can't go," I said. "The bus will be a hotbed of germs."

"I'll take a cab."

"But there may be other patients in the waiting room." I remembered it as being closet sized, with a few hard chairs jammed up against one another. "And who knows about Perez himself?" I enlisted Ann's help in trying to deter him, but all of her wheedling and warnings didn't work, either.

I don't know if he took a cab or the bus. I don't know if the waiting room was empty, as he insisted later, or if he and Dr. Perez both wore masks for the entire visit. All I know is that a little more than a week later Howard began coughing, and it wasn't one of his extravagant imaginary symptoms. He even tried to suppress it. By the next morning, he was running a fever—not that high, really, but steady. He said he didn't feel terrible and that his toe was much better. And his sense of smell was intact. You smell pretty good," he said, when I was probably rank with fear.

Dr. Ginsberg had been exposed to an infected patient at his office and was quarantining at home. A television droned in the background. "It doesn't sound too bad," he said. "He's in pretty good shape, and it could just be a run-of-the-mill flu." He paused. "But there's his age, and this other thing seems to turn on a dime. Tylenol and some Robitussin for now, but watch him, especially his breathing, and let me know."

I was a seasoned breath-watcher, so I could see and hear that Howard's had become labored even before he began to complain about it. And then his fever spiked.

"Call 911," Ginsberg said, just as I knew he would.

When the paramedics came, they put an oxygen mask over Howard's face as soon as they had him on the gurney, so that all I could see were his wide, frightened eyes. "Get his insurance cards," I was instructed. "Get his cell phone and a charger. Get him some pajamas."

"My glasses," Howard said through the mask.

I ran around looking for everything. His charger was under the bed. The only clean pajamas I could find didn't match. I hardly had a chance to think until after we'd raced down the hall and they were in the elevator and the door had slid shut between us. "Good-bye! I love you!" I called, after the fact.

The person who answered the phone in the emergency room took Howard's name and after long minutes a doctor got on. She said that he'd tested negative for Covid-19 but had pneumonia. They were going to keep him overnight for observation, but I should know that he'd been exposed to the virus there and would have to be quarantined once he got home. "Yes, yes, of course," I said. "Thank you." He didn't have it! I was manic with gratitude. I wanted to tell her she was a saint and a genius, and that I worshipped at the shrine of medicine.

Ann said, "But, Mother, how can they send him home—he has pneumonia." They called it the old man's friend. That was before antibiotics, though, wasn't it, before we were old? I began to deflate as Ann went on. How could he quarantine in our tiny apartment? Where would I sleep? I would need hired help, and that would be hard to come by in a pandemic. By the time we hung up, I was trembling.

That night Howard called on his cell phone. He was still in the emergency room; I could hear other voices behind his, like a discordant backup group, and beeping heart monitors. He said he felt like crap, but he'd eaten some of the cardboard chicken they'd given him. "Did you have dessert?" I asked—his favorite part of any meal. "Yeah, Jell-O, he said. "Your mother could have been the cook here."

I couldn't believe we were discussing food. At suppertime, I'd stood at the sink eating a sandwich, something my mother would do during a quarrel with my father, a spin-off of her famous silent treatment. Once, she didn't speak to him for an entire month, and I was enlisted to go back and forth between them with messages, like a carrier pigeon. Was that why I always talked so much? My throat ached with contained language. When I could, I said, "Hospital food, what do you expect?"

The next morning I woke up coughing. "Howie," I said, forgetting for a moment that he wasn't there. I ran my hand along his side of the bed just to be sure. The sheet was cool and smooth, but I continued speaking to him anyway, like an imbecile, like Bess Houdini. "I don't feel well," I whimpered. "What's going on?" Of course I knew the answer to that even before I sipped some tasteless coffee and tried to smell the odorless jar of Vicks.

At Dr. Ginsberg's request, they retested Howard; this time the results were positive, and his oxygen level had worsened. They were going to admit him, although there weren't any available beds yet on a medical floor. I was advised to stay home, despite the cough and the fever I now had, as long as my breathing was all right; the hospital was a madhouse and there was nothing they could do for me there anyway. I was no longer kneeling at the shrine of medicine.

Wearing a mask and gloves, I put tied trash bags just outside our apartment door. A masked and gloved stranger picked them up and left mail and the groceries my children had ordered. Sometimes I looked through the peephole just to see the back of another human being receding down the hallway. I dropped my underwear and T-shirts on the bathroom and bedroom floors and let my dirty dishes accumulate in the sink, infractions the sixties hausfrau I had been wouldn't have abided from her preteen children. I'd had to air out Jason's reeking room every day, and Ann's bed had always looked as if she were still in it.

★   ★   ★

Howard and I didn't talk about food anymore. We seemed to have entered a dual delirium. I fretted about losing my keys in the street, although I hadn't left the apartment for days. When I asked him how he felt, he said, "With my hands," and I could tell by his flat tone that he wasn't trying to make a weak joke. Maybe he believed it was a kind of cognitive test: I feel with my hands, I see with my eyes, etc., etc. He handed his phone to a doctor who introduced himself as David Chin. "I'm taking care of your husband," he said. His voice was young, yet weary. He explained that his main concern was Howard's oxygen levels, which hadn't improved. Still, he was hopeful that things would turn around. They had a malaria drug they were going to try. He took my number and promised to keep me informed.

Dr. Chin called every day at the end of his shift—things were always the same or only a little worse. "He's holding his own," was the way he put it, and then Howard would get on to say hello. He sounded like those creepy men who used to pant into the phone and then hang up. "I'm still here," he said one day. I wasn't sure if he meant in the hospital or in the world. "Me, too," I said. Dr. Chin took the phone again to ask if Howard had a living will. I wanted to come to Howard's defense for not checking off those boxes about final measures. He must have been thinking about the aroma of simmering soup, of quenching his thirst with lemonade on a summer's day. How could he renounce those simple pleasures with the stroke of a pen? Dr. Chin said, "Don't be alarmed. It's just routine."

I began to feel better, in small increments. The cough was still deep and wrenching, but less frequent, and my sense of taste and smell had returned, if not my appetite. I turned on the television news and saw the rising numbers of coronavirus cases everywhere, heard the president's cruel and cloying voice, and then the stock market report, the weather, and even a bit of entertainment news, as if things were normal.

I went into the bathroom and opened the medicine cabinet. There was that dusty bottle of citrusy cologne, years after I'd decided to simply smell like myself. Nail polish in a palette from the palest pink to the bloodiest red, and Howard's near empty can of shaving cream, his redundant bottles of antacid tablets. I dumped most of it into the wastebasket. Then I attacked the drawer in the kitchen—the crazy drawer—that was jammed with corroded batteries and takeout menus, with expired coupons and the manuals for appliances we no longer owned. Out, out!

Why had we lived this way, burdened by so much domestic clutter? I had been halfway through a literature

major at Brooklyn College when I met Howard, and he
had been that sexy thing, a jazz musician, his golden saxo-
phone an extension of his golden body. We might have
settled in Paris to pursue our artistic dreams instead of
setting up house in Queens and then Washington Heights.
We might have married other people or no one at all.
What a radical idea—obliterating our long, tumultuous
history, our indelible children and their children.

Howard needed the maximum oxygen flow, and
Dr. Chin admitted that things looked grim. Ann, who
had anguished over not being allowed to visit, told me
that she'd been speaking to Dr. Chin, too—behind my
back, I thought—and that on the brink of being attached
to a ventilator Howard had declined and signed a DNR.
"He'd never do that!" I cried. It was a mistake; maybe he
didn't understand what he was doing. But Ann assured
me that he'd been fully aware, that his dread of suffering
must have overwhelmed his dread of nothingness. "Daddy
is being brave," she said, and we wailed to each other
until one of us hung up.

Like the book club meeting and a bar mitzvah I had
recently attended, the baby shower was conducted via
Zoom. All of the gifts had been selected from a registry,

and when Abigail opened them, she and the guests in their little frames exclaimed over them in counterfeit surprise. She had told me the baby would be named for her grandfather, whom she'd adored, but that no one called a child Howard anymore. Would I mind if she just used his initial? She was thinking of Hunter or Hugo.

Dr. Chin had left word with Ann that he would be happy to speak with me whenever I was ready. I couldn't bring myself to call him. I didn't want to hear about last words or last breaths, and I let the weeks go by. Ann said that if I waited much longer, Dr. Chin might not remember Howard or me. There were so many other patients and their families, those dense pages of obituaries in the *Times* every Sunday.

I kept thinking I was beside myself. I knew it was only a figure of speech; Howard would say I was being melodramatic. In reality, I was beside no one—in our bed, on the sofa, or at the kitchen table. And Howard had died without anyone who loved him nearby, had been cremated with no one there to see him off. I hadn't witnessed any of it and my imagination failed me for once—I couldn't picture it. His clothes were hanging in the closet, his frayed blue toothbrush was in its holder. It was as if he had merely vanished, like a magician's assistant falling through a secret trapdoor.

I wouldn't let the children into the apartment yet, although I had scrubbed almost every surface with a disinfectant, and I needed their help disposing of Howard's things. We all met in the street in front of my building, wearing our disguises, and keeping the recommended distance between us—waving and blowing kisses until Jason leapt across the chasm like a caped superhero and clutched me to his heaving chest.

I left a message for Dr. Chin with his answering service, and he called me back a few hours later. "I don't know if you'll remember us—" I began, and he interrupted me. "How could I forget?" he said. "Your husband was my favorite patient." Did he tell that to all the new widows? Then he said, "Howard was such a sweet guy. He told me all about you, your whole love story, in daily installments." It didn't matter whether or not it was true. I had been shown mercy.

It's still going on—I mean the pandemic and all the rest of life. I haven't had a FaceTime visit with a psychic, and I didn't hold a Zoom séance on Howard's birthday in

October. But I often speak to him. I was hesitant and self-conscious at first, trying out a few possible code words, like his name and my own. Over time, I've become my usual garrulous self again, talking and talking about anything and everything, as if I'm goading him into answering me, if only to tell me to be quiet. So far, he hasn't.

(2020)

ACKNOWLEDGMENTS

I am deeply indebted to Henry Dunow, Nancy Miller, Elizabeth Strout, Meg Wolitzer, and Nancy Wolitzer for their faith in this book and their invaluable assistance in seeing it to fruition.

HW

A NOTE ON THE AUTHOR

HILMA WOLITZER is a recipient of Guggenheim and National Endowment for the Arts fellowships, an American Academy of Arts and Letters Award in Literature, and a Barnes & Noble Writers for Writers Award. She has taught at the Iowa Writers' Workshop, New York University, Columbia University, and the Bread Loaf Writers' Conference. Her first published story appeared when she was thirty-six, and her first novel eight years later. Her many stories and novels have drawn critical praise for illuminating the dark interiors of the American home. She lives in New York City.